HOTE[

Jane Solomon is twenty and lives in Chelsea.

HOTEL
167

JANE SOLOMON

PICADOR
Original

A Picador Original

First published 1993 by Pan Books Limited

a division of Pan Macmillan Publishers Limited
Cavaye Place London SW10 9PG
and Basingstoke

Associated companies throughout the world

ISBN 0 330 33057 8

1 3 5 7 9 8 6 4 2

A CIP catalogue record for this book is available from
the British Library

Phototypeset by Intype, London

Printed by Cox & Wyman Ltd, Reading, Berks

For Keira

Dr Ansel Grumer pulled at his beard and drew away the few bristling dead hairs. These he rolled between finger and thumb watching their flickering response. He could see the whitish nodules at the end of each where they had been rooted to his chin. He let them go, brushing his fingers together.

Swivelling his chair back round to his desk, he opened the top drawer and pulled out a manila folder. He had been enjoying the view of the Telecom Tower from his office. The Harley Street office had been his workplace for the last fifteen years and the tower had in that time become a friend. Whenever he had serious thinking to do, he looked at it as he contemplated, and enjoyed its calming effect.

Dr Grumer had refused to have double glazing in his office, unlike the others in the building. He smiled to himself, recalling to mind the decision. Although it was midwinter, the air conditioning had malfunctioned and the thermometers in the other offices read eighty degrees. Dr Grumer worked better in a cool environment and had opened the two top windows.

'Alison' – he spoke these words through the intercom to his secretary – 'could you please get Dr Bilsen on the phone for me.' Not waiting for an answer, he depressed the button and reclined, arms behind head, in his armchair.

A minute or two later the internal phone rang and he moved forward to pick up the receiver.

'Henry,' he sang out, 'I'd like to discuss the Faulkes girl

with you. Do you think you could find time to come over to the office some time today?'

Dr Bilsen was Scottish but had lived in Kent for most of his life. He commuted daily to the Wigmore Street offices from where he ran a successful psychiatric clinic.

Having been brought up in the Orient where his father had worked as British Consul and moved to Glasgow in his late childhood, his voice was a mixture of dialects. It was a definite voice, however, overly loud and scraping through the atmosphere. Dr Grumer described it to himself as a cark.

'If you're not busy, now would be the best time for me to come,' he answered, stresses on most words as the heightening pitch of his voice made them hard to differentiate.

Opening the folder absently and peering blindly at the notes that he had made, Dr Grumer nodded slowly. 'Now would be fine. I'll expect you any minute, only I've an appointment at eleven.'

Presently he fitted the telephone to its cradle and held the closed folder at eye level. He read the printed label to himself, CATHERINE MAUD FAULKES, and brought it closer to his face until he could discern the separate grey dots that made up each letter. Catherine Maud Faulkes. He read more slowly this time, sighing inwards and twitching his taut facial muscles as he did so.

In his mind he recalled the appearance of the girl. It was her eyes that had been instantly noticeable. They were large and with deep brown irises. Their colour reminded him of those of a King Charles spaniel. His first dog had been such a breed, and he remarked to himself how little else there was in common between the two pairs of eyes. It was only their colour that was comparable. The pupils of the girl had been dilated and penetrating. Not artificially though, for she took drugs, but none that would have caused such a side effect. Of course, there was no possibility that she was taking any illegal drugs either, for no one on medication would be so careless. This was what Dr Grumer thought as he waited for the arrival of his colleague.

When the door opened he raised his eyes, pulling the chair towards his desk and straightening the sheaf of letters that were awaiting his signature.

Dr Bilsen entered the room and made his way towards the now upright Dr Grumer, both extending their right hands in welcome.

'Good of you to have come,' said Grumer. Dr Bilsen nodded at this address and sat down in an armchair as he was directed. Pulling his briefcase on to his lap, he slid the locks and raised the worn leather top. Sorting through its contents, he found the notes he was looking for and, closing the case, used it as a temporary desk.

'I thought it would be easier to discuss this patient in my office rather than over the phone and by correspondence. This is not a clear case that can be easily dismissed.' Dr Grumer paused, holding a cigar box towards Bilsen, who declined the offer. 'Although you're officially retired, I didn't want to refer her to your successor without talking to you first.'

Dr Bilsen smiled with a nod of his head, not a real gesture but a diplomatic one. He liked to withhold his emotions, though he was by no means inscrutable.

With his cigar cutter, Dr Grumer lopped the end of a fat Havana and held the flame of a desk lighter to it, sucking carefully. As it lit, he puffed out, licking his lips, considering the cigar with a raised eyebrow.

3

'I only had an hour with her,' Dr Bilsen began. 'It wasn't enough to determine the root cause of her depression. She's not schizophrenic, though quite psychotic. Obsessive.' He concluded, adding, 'And very intelligent.'

'Intelligent, yes,' his colleague noted, 'but in what way specifically? Because the university was not intense enough to hold her?'

'Not only that,' the carking voice replied, 'she's a writer, you know, did you manage to get that out of her?' Waiting for a response, this time negative, he continued, 'Obsessive nature is a very common trait, a characteristic almost, of writers.'

'Coffee?' Grumer offered, indicating the percolator that stood brewing on the sideboard.

'I don't mind if I do,' was the reply and, with his hands on his desk, he pulled himself out of the chair and made his way to the glass coffee jug. Selecting two of the cups that rested down-turned on a stained doily, he turned them round on to their saucers and poured the heavy liquid in careful measures. 'Black, no sugar,' Dr Bilsen informed him, holding his hand out for the drink. Returning to the sideboard, Dr Grumer broke open two plastic pots of UHT cream and let them flow simultaneously into his cup. Next he threw in three sugar lumps and, without stirring, returned to his desk.

The two men took sips of their coffee, relaxing for a few minutes before continuing their meeting.

'She never smiles,' noted Dr Grumer thoughtfully. 'Hardly ever,' he corrected.

'The medication has made her put on quite a lot of weight,' Dr Bilsen added for his part, 'she told me she was quite thin before. She has been anorexic.'

'Most girls have,' Grumer snorted under his breath, 'the

middle classes especially, but I think that is changing a little now.'

'Yes, I looked up the Flupenthixol, that does cause swelling, particularly of the tongue, the face and the breasts.'

'The tongue, face and breasts...' Grumer considered, repeating the words of his friend. 'Yes, I noticed the face was a little puffy. The waist was thickened perhaps too. And the breasts. Yes, they were heavy. Like small water balloons.' He smiled nostalgically. 'I remember that game from when I was a young boy. We filled balloons with water and threw them at each other. Did you play that game?' he asked, interested.

'I think we all did,' Bilsen answered. 'Water bombs... Her face was flushed, I did notice that as well.'

'The Amitriptyline has that side effect, of course,' Grumer reminded him. 'Yes, I wanted you to see her, because of her physical appearance as well. I think it's so interesting,' he continued, moving forward with his elbows on the desk, 'to see how the mental illness carries on into the appearance of the person. Yes, at one point I moved towards her, to look at some scars on her arm,' Grumer licked his lips and brought the coffee to his mouth, taking sips, 'and I could distinguish a variety of smells. Body odour, but not only that, the smell of stale antiperspirant and also the gum that she chewed. The sweat and the deodorant were most noticeable. A dark body odour. It filled the nose.'

Dr Bilsen drew his chair closer.

'Tell me about the scars,' he was asked. 'All that she told me was that she had made them with razor blades.'

He paused before answering and when he did, there was a controlled eagerness in his voice. 'Yes, the scars were most interesting. She seemed pleased to be questioned about them, proud almost. She told me that a friend of hers had been excited by them, because the marks were a tattoo. When I looked at them, they were faint, all the way from the wrist to the elbow. Unusually, they were not on the veined side of the arm.' Clearing his throat, he continued, 'She answered my questions readily, told me that they were more visible in the cold, that they turned a pale shade of purple. She looked at me as she spoke, awaiting my reaction it seems.'

'But you showed none,' Grumer offered.

'Exactly. I did not want her to be immediately satisfied. Next she told me that she enjoyed the cutting, not as a form of masochism or more commonly as a way of invoking reality, and feeling, but as a hobby.'

'Interesting.' Grumer was pleased at this detail.

'I thought so. When she spoke of the blades I noticed the high colour in her cheeks, seeping to the edges of her ears. She described the process by which she purchased the blades, trying out new makes, once a platinum edge, another time a double-sided blade. Then she spoke of the different smells of the metal edges. Particularly of the Gillette razor blade. I have since experienced the metallic odour that she described as "hairy". She found it quite a sexual smell.'

Dr Grumer inhaled deeply. 'What else?' he asked.

Bilsen looked at his acquaintance, noticing the perspiration droplets at the edges of his eyebrows, close to the temples. He brought his attention back to the subject in question and thought deeply for a few moments.

'Apparently, the process of cutting is to her a hobby. Not something that she carries out for the burning sensation that the blade makes, not either because of the ensuing blood. Merely, she enjoys the buying of the blade and the secrecy of the cutting. At the time she told no one about it. Even now she does not use it as a form of exhibitionism. She does not hide it because it is so visible. The scars are so profuse that it would be foolish to make up excuses for their presence. So she treats it as something in her past, something interesting but unimportant.' Bilsen looked directly at Grumer, waiting for his reaction.

'So,' Grumer began. 'She does not do it for the frisson?' he tempted.

Bilsen shook his head.

'But for most people, this would be the underlying reason, wouldn't it?' he suggested, heaving himself up from the chair. He made his way contemplatively round the room, pausing at a painting of a shire horse in harness. 'Yes, for you or me,' he suggested, 'there would be a frisson, would there not?' and saying this, he placed his hands on the back of Bilsen's chair, feeling the hard wood beneath his fingers, rubbing them over its varnished surface. Bilsen reclined and Grumer extricated his fingers from behind the strong back of his friend.

'I think that, perhaps there would,' Bilsen admitted, rewarded as Grumer transferred his hands to his shoulders, massaging them sensitively.

Bilsen arched his neck.

'What did she tell you about her sexual experiences?' he was asked.

'Very interesting, quite unusual,' was the answer. 'She told me everything, and the truth I am sure.' Bilsen arched his neck and continued: 'When she was seven, she was kissed by a stranger. Standing in the front garden of her house, she gave directions to an Italian stranger, the garden wall separating the both of them. He grabbed at her neck and she felt sure she was going to be strangled.' Bilsen clutched at his own neck, at the fingers of his friend already clasped there.

'She was not strangled, though,' he went on, 'the man pressed his mouth to hers and forced his tongue into her mouth.'

Bilsen tilted his head back further until he was staring at Grumer, studying his eyes. The other doctor brought his head down closer and then his mouth was pressed on the other's and each tongue searched the other out.

Grumer broke away roughly; his breath hardened.

'What else?' he asked, swivelling Bilsen round in his chair so that they were face to face.

Bilsen's voice was unchanged: 'She has only had sexual intercourse once.'

'Once,' Grumer repeated.

Bilsen nodded. 'With a bisexual lover,' he added.

'A male lover or a female lover?' He was then asked.

'A male lover.'

Grumer unzipped his trousers and pulled out his member. Bilsen saw that it was hard and erect. Grumer began to masturbate until Bilsen put his hands over the penis and helped his friend.

'Our Maud has been masturbating since she was two or three,' Bilsen proffered to the fast-breathing Grumer. 'And having orgasms too.' At this point Grumer enjoyed his own, taking care to direct himself into his pocket handkerchief, and away from his friend's suit. The handkerchief was a present from his wife. It was a pale blue floral design from Liberty's that matched his tie.

When he washed it out and hung it to dry on the window ledge, it faded to leave no stain.

The girl looked up, wiping the cranny of her lip with her finger.

'Sorry, could you repeat the question?' she asked.

The doctor looked at her. 'Do you fantasize about your psychiatrists?'

She paused. 'No,' she replied, vaguely shaking her head.

The psychiatrist leant back slightly in his chair, clasping his hands with the forefingers meeting at a point.

'Do you masturbate?' he enquired.

'Yes,' Catherine Maud Faulkes answered without the embarrassment of thought.

'When did you start masturbating?' He continued the questioning.

'Since I was two or three,' Maud said, still not allowing herself to think, distancing herself from such questions.

'Two or three,' the psychiatrist repeated; 'and do you have orgasms?'

'Yes.'

'Have you always had orgasms?' the doctor was keen to know.

'Since I was two or three, yes!' Maud could not keep the subtle mixture of embarrassment and pride from the edge of her voice. 'Is that strange?' she asked, trying to detract from the tone of her previous answer.

He breathed inwards, then looked straight at her: 'There are no statistics for girls,' he said. 'From the age of fourteen, ninety-six per cent of boys masturbate. But girls sometimes start

at that age, sometimes much later or earlier. Some never dis-
cover masturbation at all. It's hard to put into figures.'

'Interesting,' Maud added, allowing herself to relax.

'Could you tell me how your mind was at first affected?'
The doctor renewed his questioning on a different topic.

Maud concentrated hard, thinking back to her gap year,
when she had worked for her parents.

'I spent almost the whole of the year before university on
my own. I worked with my parents, of course, but saw almost
nobody else. There are no young people in their office.' Again
she paused, collecting her thoughts, allowing them time to
assimilate, to coagulate. Maud smiled nervously, unsure of the
doctor's reception to her answer. She cleared her throat preparatorily.

'Well, it depends; the things changed as the year progressed:
when the natural light altered.' Maud pulled the sleeves of her
sweater down, over her hands. She could feel the wool soak up
the sweat that lay in the ridges of her palms. Holding her breath
silently, she concentrated, violently amassing her thoughts. The
silence was heavy and demanding; it made her cringe.

'On the left-hand side of the Old Brompton Road, in the
Earl's Court direction,' she began, 'there were houses with deep
basements . . .' Pausing, listening for a reaction and meeting
silence, she continued: 'The basements were damp and cold,
but it was summertime and this drew me. They were fairly
bare. Usually there was a patchy flower-bed overgrown with
nasturtium leaves. That was quite important. And there might
be an upside-down flower pot and sometimes a white wrought-
iron bench. Some of the basements had moss growing through
the cracks between the York stone paving.'

At this point Maud looked up, but the doctor's eyes met

hers and he did not speak. She continued her explanation. 'Then there was the Citroën van. It's an old make, an odd shape like a laundry van. Perhaps that's what it was. It was a blue-ridged vehicle with the metal Citroën arrowheads on its nose. It used to stop at various points along the other side of the Old Brompton Road. That was also more important to me than it should have been.'

The doctor pressed his lips together as he finished taking his notes. Then he looked up, smiling faintly.

'What would happen to you if you didn't see these things?' he asked.

'Nothing really,' Maud replied, 'it just used to make me happy to see them. More happy than my life would have been without them. They were the most important things in my day at that time.' Tilting her head to one side, 'I would become anxious until I saw them. There were other things too,' she concluded.

'Obsessional thoughts are fairly common,' the doctor observed. 'I could give you a capsule to overcome them,' he went on. 'You would only have to take one at bedtime. A very helpful drug. Stelazine, it's called.'

Maud thought for a moment. 'I'm taking two types of drug already, I'd really rather not take any more.'

'You could take it instead of the Flupenthixol,' the doctor hurriedly added. 'You'd still only be taking two, and it would clear your head of those thoughts that are upsetting you.'

'Oh, they're not upsetting,' Maud challenged, in defence of her obsessional thoughts. 'I'm not sure that I want to get rid of them,' she explained, 'I'd rather have those thoughts than none at all.'

Maud slouched into the back of her chair, dampened by

the possibility of losing those thoughts that had kept her alive for a whole year.

The thoughts that had been her friends during her enforced solitariness.

The doctor was sympathetic. 'I can understand how you feel, but perhaps your mind would become clear for other thoughts. More normal ones, that wouldn't have such a hold over you.'

'But I've got used to the thoughts, I'll have to think about it,' Maud contested, frustrated that this was all the doctor could do to help her.

The doctor stood up, taking a flash at his watch.

'Right. I think that's all,' he said, 'I'll be writing to your GP about our meeting, if you could make an appointment with his secretary, to see him.'

He smiled and Maud got to her feet, taking the strap of her shoulder-bag that lay against the legs of her chair.

He opened the door. 'Thank you,' she said, hovering on the threshold. The doctor held out his hand and Maud shook it, aware of the dampness of her palm against his dry professional one.

'Goodbye,' they spoke at each other and Maud walked down the corridor to the front door and out into the street, numbed. The workmen repairing a section of the pavement seemed incongruous in the light of her experience.

Physically emptied, Maud felt that her innards were exposed to the passers by. She resented the doctor's abruptness, wishing that he had made some sign to her before ending the session.

She wondered whether he had asked her some of the questions merely to test her reaction, to see if there was embarrassment. Thankfully, this was the fourth psychiatrist that she had been to and she knew enough of their ways not to let them manipulate her for their personal pleasure. Half smiling to herself, she congratulated her performance, although indignant at the doctor's treatment of her.

In the distance Maud could see the reassuring John Lewis building. Accordingly, she walked in that direction, determined to draw comfort from the reality of the department store and the partnership of its staff.

Crossing the road to the shop's back entrance, Maud pushed the heavy glass door and walked through. She held it open momentarily in case there was anyone behind and then made her way through the inner door and into the static environment. There was a sense of security to be found in the heavy carpeting, the pile worn smooth by customers' soles. Maud made her way across the ground floor to the haberdashery section, past where the shelving was filled with long rolls of materials.

A length of fabric hung loose from each roll and she enjoyed running her hand along, feeling for the different textures. The diaphanous floral patterns ran across her fingers and she let herself forget the morning's ordeal. Today she loved the thin flowery viscose, although the patterns and colours were overpowering and poorly matched.

Further along, there were shelved cans of shoulder pads. Taking one down Maud pulled the lid off and peered at the foamy contents before returning it to the gap it had left.

On display, there were heavy dummies with smooth silhouettes, svelte in different sizes. Bust to hips, each stood on a metal rod, two halves screwed together so that the measurements could be increased.

Next to these a saleswoman, surrounded on all sides by boards of buttons and buckles all tied into place. Maud turned the circumference, her eyes closely skimming the gilt and plastic shapes secured by metal wire. There were card strips of pre-packaged buttons too in sixes and eights; best sellers that would end up on hand-knitted cardigans worn by grandchildren and nieces. Maud spun the revolving stand, mutely watching the varying coloured eyes.

Past the haberdashery section, on the same floor, was the jewellery department. There were salesgirls at each counter, chatting to each other with one eye on the clients who tried on the bracelets and chains, making use of the mirrors that stood on each surface.

A man on a stepladder was repairing the lighting, and Maud enjoyed the anonymity that the darkness lent. The electrician had removed one of the ceiling panels and was checking the complicated wiring for short circuits.

'What's happened with the lights. Who's turned them off?' an old woman in a furry Kangol hat asked, prodding Maud at the shoulder.

Maud smiled. 'There's something wrong with them, look,' and she pointed to the electrician, 'they've obviously turned the lot off while he fixes them.'

'Oh, I see,' was the woman's response as she moved on, uninterested.

Maud turned over the price tag of one of the pearl neck-laces. Although made of plastic, the unevenness of the beads was quite cleverly done. Maud disliked fakes. The clasp was a gilt shape, like an unprinted Roman coin. She thought it looked like a chewed toffee. Smiling to herself, she unhooked it from the metal loop and held it in her fist. A section of the string of beads hung free, but the shop assistants were busy chatting and no one noticed.

14

Nothing more was of interest to Maud, so she made her way through the swing doors and out of the back exit.

It was in her first term of university that Maud discovered cutting. At the beginning of the second term at Bristol University she had to leave for reasons of health.

The doctor's certificate had read 'Maud Faulkes will be suffering for depression for six months', and when she read it she was filled with the irony of this sentencing.

It is true to say that the cutting began in the first term at university, although she was not actually in the city of Bristol at that time. Because of her depression, she had travelled down to London, where it had been organized for her to see a psychiatrist at the Lodge Park Hospital.

Maud had, some years previously, read a magazine article about cutting. Articles about psychological problems regularly appear in women's magazines and this was how she was first introduced to the symptom.

Maud had made two friends during her time at Bristol; one during the first half of the term, and another just before she had left. She was no longer in contact with Sophie, the first girl with whom she had become acquainted; Sophie had been unable to cope with the abrupt mood changes and depressing attitude of her friend. Maud felt that she had been deserted, but in reality Sophie had had a lot to cope with on her own, it being her first term too, and had taken more pleasure in mixing with livelier people.

Sophie had, however, suffered a similar bout of depression only a year before. She had recovered quickly, but it was through her that Maud made her first direct contact with cutting.

Once, while they talked to each other of their pasts, Sophie had admitted that she had tried cutting herself; she had even shown Maud the faint white marks close to her wrist where the razor blade had scarred.

When she was in London, Maud found herself tempted by this idea and the secrecy that would ensue.

On her way to the chemist, she was preoccupied with the object of this errand and found herself enjoying the planning.

There were several types of blades available, some of them Boots' own brand, but Maud dismissed these; they seemed to detract from the romanticism of the pilgrimage.

In the end she chose a pack of ten Wilkinson Sword double-edged razor blades. She returned home with her purchase, quite surprised at how expensive such an item was.

Sitting at the kitchen table, Maud tore the plastic surround from the cardboard backing. The pack of blades came free in her hand and she slid one out. It was covered in a waxed printed paper. Holding this to the light, she could make out the shape of the metallic blade inside.

Unfolding the paper, she took out the blade and examined it for a few moments. She liked the brand-new shine of the stainless steel and the carefully chiselled edge.

Testing it carefully on the back of her arm, she drew it across lightly so that it burned but left only a faint mark like that of a scratch.

It took about fifteen minutes before she felt comfortable enough with the blade. She was constantly aware, though, of the excitement she felt at this new experience. It was a novelty, rendered even more so by the prospect of blood.

Placing the blade edge firmly on to her skin, she scored very slowly along her arm. Holding her breath as she did, she was surprised at the quality of the pain. An intense burning, nothing more.

When the score was long enough, she withdrew the blade. At first all that was visible was a white line, a fairly deep white line. It took a few seconds before the first red beads began to emerge and then only like the heads of cyclists over a hill. Soon the beads joined together, the red of a jam doughnut centre, and then there was a slow trickle down the arm, to which Maud held her tongue.

The results although satisfying were at the same time addictive. The cut was comparable to the artist's initial drawing for a repetitive design. Not something that had unique appeal, but that would thrive among identical images.

Maud worked down her arm until there were four or five cuts and a steady flow of blood. Soon the cuts became something edifying, a visible embodiment of her feelings. She was able to nurse her arm as she would like to have nurtured her brain, to apply a tissue to mop up the blood, to massage in antiseptic cream. She drew her sweater down her arm, taking care not to brush past the wound.

She had cut herself enough for that day, but only for that day. The next time she was thus tempted was soon enough for the cuts not to have healed. It was in this way that her arm became covered from the elbow to the wrist in vibrant red lines, varying in stages of clotting and scabbing.

The first time that Maud thought of the sexual connotation of the cutting process was when she had purchased a packet of Gillette blades. Immediately she noticed that they smelled different from the Wilkinson Sword blades.

Holding a blade close to her nose, Maud inhaled heavily and again and again until she had become immune to the smell and had to breathe for a minute or so to clear it from her nostrils and her brain.

The Gillette smell was hairy, a metallic masculine hair smell. It was acidic enough to be an attractive smell and she took a more intense pleasure in using this variety because of the added sense involved.

Maud continued this practice while she was at university, at first keeping it a secret from the rest of the girls on her corridor. She had to be careful, because she would instinctively and obsessively roll up her sleeve to check the progress of her cuts. She would tire of the cutting, tell herself that she must let them heal finally and then suffer an intense frustration and break her promise. It was not long before the cutting became in itself a frustrating preoccupation and then Maud ceased to pander to herself. She felt that there was a separate part of her that was carrying out the abuse to her arm. She would become angry at it. She would be threatening and it was not long before she betrayed it and revealed its wickedness to the new friend, Vivien. She had spoken to her only once a few days before and now she was desperate to off-load pent-up emotions to another. 'I'm sick of myself,' was her first self-taunt, 'and I refuse to let myself get away with it any longer.'

Vivien stared at her, unsure of what her own response should be, and therefore remaining silent.

'I've been anorexic, bulimic, I've started cutting myself. There's no way it's getting away with it, there will be no more pandering or preoccupation,' and she emphasized these words with the side of her hand.

Vivien was to forget these words as soon as they had been spoken, there was too much drama for her to take any real notice; but Maud was soon able to share her experiences of cutting with the new friend and thought this would help her to break the physical and psychological addiction.

Vivien found Maud's accounts entertaining, and a little alarming at first. The first time that she saw the cuts she was impressed and taken aback. She would often accuse Maud of being crazy. 'You're crazy!' she would say, but Maud it must be stressed was not seeking pity or interest in herself. She was merely tired of the secrecy and the self-blackmail that went on between herself and her arm.

It was particularly hard for Maud to give up cutting because of Billy the blunt blade. The naming of a much used and now disabled blade was dangerous in that it created a relationship between herself and the inanimate blade. Of course she didn't like the blade so much when it was in the characterless and passive state, and this was one of the difficulties that she had. This was overcome, however, by an exercise of purgation. Maud was aware that another of Vivien's friends suspected the cutting and realized the more people knew, the harder it would be to continue. Even if it was all paranoia on her part. Thus it was that she created a collage that took its place by the corridor's pay-phone on the landing; a picture of a model obscured by a second layer so that only her body from breast to hips was visible as if cut out by the razor blades that hovered near by. It was entitled *Modesty Blades* after a cartoon strip of a voluptuous double agent. Maud only removed it indignantly several weeks later when someone stuck a passport photograph of a male student above the body.

When the doctor had asked to see the scars on Maud's arm, he had expressed a personal dislike for the habit, describing it as 'a messy symptom'. It was not one that he liked his patients to pursue and Maud felt that he had dismissed it unfairly, without trying to understand her motivations.

Back at the university, she and Vivien had taken a bottle of vodka back to one of the rooms. Neither of them spent much time in the Hall bar and they felt that they deserved relief from the university life. A male colleague of Vivien's from the branch of McDonald's where she worked part time had joined them. On becoming drunk, Vivien was driven to the sexual pursuit of her friend. Maud had rushed down to her room to collect her familiar blades and on returning began to cut her arm. There was an ironic contrast between the two girls' attitudes and the next day Vivien awoke to a smear of blood on the wall above her bed.

When Maud thought back to Dr Grumer's appointment with her, she began to resent the way he had treated her practices as commonplace. He seemed to exclude the possibility of his patients' individuality. To him, they seemed to differ only in the permutations of the symptoms that they suffered from. It was because of the questioning that Maud had recently been subjected to that forgotten memories had begun to be restored. This, too, was upsetting for her. When the question of sexuality arose, she began to wonder whether she had not had experiences as a child that remained lodged in her subconscious. Since she was two or three, she had used a name to describe the act of masturbation. Until later years, she had not paid much attention to the reason behind this. It seemed natural and unquestionable.

Now, however, she began to piece together clues that floated to the front of her mind and drove her beliefs. Realizing that the name she had assigned was the same as that of an early friend's dog, she began to wonder whether she had in fact been abused by the child's father. She felt that if there wasn't any certainty of this being the case, then she surely would never have made the connection.

Moreover, for the first ten years of her life, Maud had been terrified of kites. This seemed to confirm her suspicions, the kitchen of her friend's house having been papered with a kite design. The more she thought of it, the more certain she needed to be. She could not now put the idea out of her mind until it was confirmed one way or the other.

If she had never asked for psychiatric help, these secrets, true or false, would have remained in the past. It was not that Maud blamed the doctor for the light that had been thrown on her past. Simply she felt that the sessions were too one-sided. She recalled how the doctor had subtly worked the sleeve of his shirt up, in order that he might keep an eye on the time. As soon as the hour was over, he managed to wind the conversation up with professionalism. It was only when she was shown out of the door that Maud realized the efficiency of the doctor's forward planning.

It was therefore not on purpose that Maud had kept her greatest love a secret; her obsession with the hotel: Yes! Hotel 167.

Hotel 167 was situated on the left side of the Old Brompton Road in the Earl's Court direction. Faintly Tunisian in style, Hotel 167 was the landmark of primary importance to Maud. It had been during her gap year, when she walked to work and back every day. Although Maud had no real understanding of the importance of the building, she would work herself up until she finally passed it. She could still recreate the combined surge of awe and happiness that filled her on seeing the hotel. Painted a medium mint green, with a black sign and miniature palm trees in their window-box, the hotel was incongruous in the light of the rest of the buildings. It was continental, even the lamps that Maud could see when she peered into the rest room did not fit in with the Earl's Court aura! The lamps were opaque bowls on long stems, lit very faintly and art nouveau in style.

Maud smiled as she thought of the great power that she had over all the psychiatrists that she had been to. This confidence was not something brought about as a result of the violation that she felt was taking place in her mind. Simply she had never been able to see the doctors as people who were blessed with the ability to help those who mentally offered themselves up.

Maud was very much aware of the way she was treated by the men. It was for this reason that she had not wanted to be helped by a female doctor. Understandably, from her point of view, she feared that a woman would compare her with her own stability of mind; criticize her because they would be on a level with each other. A male doctor could not claim to understand the workings of a female mind. And Maud knew that she always needed this protection. She would gain from the experiences in as much as the psychiatrist could act as a father figure to her. He was better than a parent, because he could never apportion her blame. He would always be interested in her interpretation of life. He, only, would ask the questions; he could not therefore demand anything of her. Except for truth of course. This was where Maud's idea of her own power lay. She could control her own input and reward the doctor accordingly. His understanding she interpreted as a way of begging for information. There was no help. She had learned that from the first experience she had had of an NHS psychiatrist, while she was in Bristol.

Maud had gone to her GP to ask for help. She felt that the act of leaving university, especially after only the first term, would cause herself, and all those with expectations of her, a great deal of pain. There were some people, certain friends and family members, whom she did not want to upset. Others, her competitors, she did not want to have the satisfaction of seeing her fail. It was with this in mind that she first made an appointment to be referred to a psychiatrist, a doctor, someone who would help.

This initial attempt was an abortive experience.

She was prescribed anti-depressants, referred to a counsellor and finally told, a week or so later, that there was no place for her.

When she made a second appointment, unable physically to attend her tutorials, Maud was given an appointment with a psychiatrist at the nearby Southam Hospital.

The appointment was not immediate and during this waiting time, she found it easier to cope. The prospect of being given treatment, having her depression off-loaded on to someone else, experiencing catharsis, temporarily restored her will.

Several days prior to the appointment, Maud asked Vivien to make a call to the hospital; they decided that Vivien would pretend to call from the University Health Centre, requesting to speak to the doctor in question, thereby ascertaining his or her gender.

The plan worked, as Maud and Vivien wrongly thought, because of their combined prowess, their contrivance. This is how the conversation went:

Vivien: 'Hello, extension 446 please . . . Could I please speak to Dr Fellows, this is the University Health Centre (*muffled laughter in the background*) . . . I need to verify the correct spelling of his name. We appear to have two Dr Fellows on our list . . . Hello? Dr Fellows (*laughter, line cut off*) . . . Hello, sorry

I was trying to get hold of Dr Fellows, the line was cut off . . . Dr Fellows, could you spell out your surname and Christian names, please . . .'

Of course, the secretary of this psychiatric consultant should have been more careful than to have put the call through, especially the second time. The psychiatric consultant shouldn't have given such information so liberally either.

However, that is not entirely relevant to the point that is being made; the lack of intelligence of the hospital's co-ordinators and particularly of its resident doctors.

At least she now knew that Dr Fellows was male. She needed to know that much in advance. Just so she knew what to expect; it made her feel one step ahead of him; at least, she knew something that he didn't know that she knew.

Southam Hospital was in Westbury-on-Trym, several miles away from the city centre. Maud walked down to where she knew that a fleet of parked black cabs waited for passengers. She approached the first car and opened the rear door.

'Where to?' the driver asked, looking at her in his rear-view mirror.

'Southam Hospital please,' she replied, hauling herself into the back seat and delving into her pocket to sort out the fare money from the assortment of half-used lipsticks, chewing gum, wrappers and matchboxes.

Maud studied the route that the driver took, in order that she would be able to walk back after her appointment. She went everywhere by foot and therefore hadn't travelled far afield. Westbury-on-Trym was flatter than the areas Maud was used to and consequently much windier. The parts of Bristol that she frequented were more heavily populated and generally more opulent. The shops that the car passed were mostly charity shops and bargain stores. Maud was surprised, however, to pass an expensive-looking health shop brimming with customers. She supposed that the people felt that they were entitled to spend money on their health even if they couldn't afford more basic needs.

The hospital, she saw when they arrived, was incomplete and there was a churning mixer preparing cement for the builders busy grouting a new section of walling.

Maud slid to the door and pushed her way out of the low-seated car. Having paid the driver, she watched as he made a U-turn and disappeared out of sight.

There were no people outside the bungalow-like buildings that made up the hospital. Maud followed the sign that read PSYCHIATRIC UNIT and arrived at one of the bungalows; pushing the door, she made her way to the reception desk and gave her name.

'Maud Faulkes. I've an appointment with Dr Fellows,' she said, and was shown with a smile to the waiting area where a circle of easy chairs surrounded a low coffee table with newspapers and magazines.

There were two other people waiting when Maud sat down. She couldn't help thinking how depressed the woman nearest her looked. Further away, sitting on one of a second circle of chairs, was a youth. He looked completely passive; just sat waiting. He didn't even seem to have thoughts crossing behind his eyes.

Glancing outside the window, Maud watched three builders busy constructing a new section of the hospital. There was a pile of cement on the ground and a few vans combined as temporary housing.

It was about twenty minutes before a young man appeared

and asked her to follow him. Hitching her bag across her shoulder, she obeyed, and was led into a small room with a couple of chairs and a desk.

'I'm going to conduct an interview with you before you meet with Dr Fellows,' the man explained. 'I'm Geoffrey,' he introduced himself.

Maud felt strange talking to the man. He was only in his early thirties and asked her if she minded him drinking coffee. She wondered whether this was a trick question, a test for the prospective patient. She wondered how the others had responded. When he swallowed there was a loud liquid noise. Too much saliva. She wondered that the amylase didn't begin to digest the roof of his mouth.

The actual questions in this interview were only slightly different from those of other occasions that she had experienced.

He did ask her if she was breast fed, though, and when she replied in the negative, he asked her why she thought that was.

'Because my mother didn't have enough milk,' she answered with difficulty. The question was a deliberate attempt to make her aware of the accidental rejection of herself when she was young. It hadn't been her mother's fault that she had no breast milk. Why did he have to make it seem like her mother didn't want her leaching from her? Or perhaps he wanted her to think that it was her fault that there wasn't any milk. Or perhaps it was. She began to dislike the young man whose looks were insipid and never to be remembered when at last she left his company. She could, however, remember the mousiness of his hair, and the slurping saliva swallow.

'Could you return to the waiting area now. I'm just going to consult with Dr Fellows, and then I'll call you back when both of us will be present.'

Again Maud obeyed his directions, you see she had to because she had been waiting for the appointment for two weeks and she knew that she had to go along with what they told her or she wouldn't be helped.

She was trying not to be negative, she was hopeful that Dr Fellows would have something to tell her, that it would be the answer to everything that was going on in her life. Not that she knew what was going on, but maybe at least the confusion would be dissipated by this meeting.

Again the man called her, and once more she followed him, this time into a different room, just opposite the previous one.

'This is Dr Fellows.' The young man indicated the consultant to Maud, who in turn shook his extended hand with a 'How do you do.'

Dr Fellows' eyes, she noticed, were too close set. They were hard, a hard hazelnut colour and a hard hazelnut shape. There was a mole on his cheek just across from his mouth and with premonition she felt her hopes subside.

'Geoffrey has relayed to me the information that you gave him and we're trying to decide how best to help you. Have you suggestions?'

Maud thought this questioning about treatment strange, and she said as much: 'If I knew how I could be helped, I probably wouldn't have come,' she explained, finding the threesome situation trying.

'Well, why did you come then?' was his question.

'I thought you might be able to help me,' she replied, puzzled as to the direction of this questioning.

'Well, we can't help you until we know how. Have you any suggestions?'

Maud paused. 'If I knew what types of treatment were available, then yes, perhaps I could tell you how to proceed.'

'There is no treatment available!' said Dr Fellows, emphasizing with the use of hand movement.

'Well, if you aren't going to help me, then I'll just have to go away and help myself.'

'There is no help on offer,' reiterated Dr Fellows, raising his voice.

Maud watched his eyes, but it was not in these that his anger was displayed. They were too dead to be indicative of his emotions.

'I don't understand,' Maud explained, by now confused. 'You asked me if I wanted help.'

'I said there is no help on offer. We are not going to offer you help unless you tell us what your problem is.' Dr Fellows was almost rising from his seat with anger.

Perplexed, Maud made another attempt. 'If I knew what the problem is I wouldn't have come,' she said.

'So you admit there is no problem,' said Fellows.

'I said I don't know,' repeated Maud.

'Then I'll write to your GP and say that you don't think you have a problem,' he ended rising and walking towards the door, which he opened.

'Then you're a crap psychiatrist,' Maud voiced her opinion, walking out.

'Bye,' said the young man, who had made no attempt to bring the two of them together in understanding each other. She could hardly reply.

Walking out into the low windy sky, Maud felt frustration tugging at her throat, taunting her. It was as if Dr Fellows had deliberately tried to upset her so that she should not receive the treatment that she deserved. The build-up to the appointment had been of primary importance to her. It was what made that section of her life matter. If there had been no potential meeting, what would Maud have used to look forward to, to keep her from going mad?

Concentrating her mind back to the morning's drive from Clifton to Westbury-on-Trym, Maud tried to recall the route that the black cab had taken. There only seemed one direction that she could take, so she followed the poorly built road, stopping at the first newsagent's to buy some gum.

Most of the shops along that road were newsagents'. The first Indian newsagent's and corner shops that she had seen in Bristol. On arriving in the city, she had been struck by how few people of ethnic minorities she came across. She found herself staring when she saw an Indian woman, baby strapped to her front, crossing the road. It was only a matter of time though, and she dismissed the thought.

After an hour's walking, Maud stopped and asked a woman for directions. Unable to tell her how to get to Clifton, she did guide her to the Broadmead shopping centre and from there Maud knew her way.

She stopped off at a smaller branch of McDonald's in Broadmead. Vivien was working there that day and had been urging her to pay a visit for some time. Pushing through the heavy swing door and holding it open for the woman with the pushchair behind her, she made her way to the tills at the back.

Taking her place behind two women with children, she watched as Vivien took their order, aware that she was oblivious to Maud's presence. As she turned to fill up a waxed cup with milkshake, Maud took in the full appearance of her friend's uniform. The slim pants suited Vivien's sleek figure and unusually she had tied her brown hair in a high ponytail which swished through the back of the red cap. Vivien had been brought up in Brussels and had been educated in a *lycée* where she had taken the baccalaureate. She seemed more American than continental, though, and suited the McDonald's restaurant better than her counterparts. Vivien grinned when Maud finally caught her attention.

'Hi, so you finally made it.' She greeted Maud in her scratchy mid-continental/American accent.

'I'll have a diet Coke.' Maud felt less at ease in the fast-food environment than her friend.

'How was Dr Fellows?' Vivien grinned at the mutual joke that had begun the evening that they contacted him on behalf of the University Health Centre.

'Oh, it was a completely abortive trip.' Maud looked behind, aware of the growing queue, and stepped aside.

'Wait there a moment,' Vivien called to her as she began serving a tall man clutching a carrier-wrapped soft toy.

Presently, the queue of customers lifted and Vivien was again free to talk.

'You look really professional behind the counter.' There was surprise in Maud's voice.

'Really?' Her friend was pleased at the compliment. 'So, what happened?'

Maud sighed. 'He was a complete schmuck, I had to talk to the guy under him, and when I finally met him, we started to argue. I called him a crap psychiatrist and walked out . . .'

'Cool,' Vivien interjected.

Maud shook her head. She was not pleased at the way she had behaved that morning. Staying on at the university was dependent on her getting some form of treatment while in Bristol. Of all the doctors she had ever dealt with, never had she lost her temper and insulted one. Already she was aware that leaving Bristol was imminent, if only so that she could be referred to a different psychiatrist.

Taking her drink, she unwrapped a thick straw and slid it through the hole in the top. The plastic made a deep bowing noise as it pushed through the punctured lid.

Once out of the McDonald's Maud walked aimlessly along the pedestrian shopping precinct, and into the main mall that had opened only a few months previously. Only half of the shops were as yet open and in the last couple of months she had looked in each one. There seemed nothing left for her in Bristol. Apart from Clifton and Broadmead, there was little else to see. The trips to Broadmead had become part of Maud's daily routine and she felt that her life was limited because of the city's restrictions. Throwing the empty cup into one of the council-maintained rubbish bins, she began to walk away from Broadmead and back through Clifton, towards the Hall.

Now that Maud was in London, she couldn't understand how she had managed to cope in Bristol for so long. Her arm was healed. The cuts had been sealed with new skin and were only faintly visible. London seemed so much freer, not just because of the Underground, or the difference in size, but because of the attitudes of those who lived there. They seemed to have more purpose, more ambition than the people of Bristol. Life was carried out at a faster pace, people were less aware of the fact that they were alive for they did not concentrate on this. They merely did what they had to do, lived actively instead of indirectly, through the media and through their jobs, through stories and gossip. There was, above all, anonymity in London. You could frequent the same newsagent's daily, and although you would be recognized, nothing would

31

be thought of it, most of all you yourself thought nothing of it. In Bristol, Maud had been so aware of her movements, passing student after student in the main areas of the city, looking down so that she could be excused a response if noticed, greeted. She felt a heel because of the way she behaved. Here, she knew no one cared and this thought was liberating.

There was the question, however, of the hotel. Hotel 167.

As she thought to herself, Maud breathed in deeply, filling her lungs agreeably. She enjoyed the wholeness that Hotel 167 lent her. She felt its stability transfer to her. She knew they were connected, though not why. Shunning the idea of her finding a spiritual closeness with the building, because of the implications of this type of ideology, Maud could not but accept that this must be true. Laughing at herself, this was the first time for many months that she had been able to do so. Was it London, or was it her closeness with 167 that made her feel this way, purged her thoughts that had lain putrefying for so long? Perhaps it was not so much real, more to do with the respect she had created in her mind for the hotel. A mutual respect that was immune to the pressure of others that she often felt compounded her brain. There was a secure oasis, small but sincere, that was her reward for not allowing the doctors and analysts and psychiatrists into the whole of her thinking. Although they had emptied her emotionally, made her feel naked mentally, and we all know this was more powerful than any physical degradation, she had retained something. All the more important for the difficulty she had experienced in doing so. This ground had become hallowed, although Maud treated it with the jocundity and half spiritedness that was necessary for it to remain so.

The darkly fleshed eyelids of Dr Ansel Grumer winced lightly in concentration. Beneath the fine-lined skins, the movement of his eyeballs was apparent. There was a rapid shifting, horizontal in movement, as they appeared to focus on the interns of his mind. His head, however, remained coolly placed on the plain sheeting of his pillow. It was an anatomical pillow that he had sent off for from a mail-order catalogue and it moulded to the position of his head and neck. He slept alone.

The furnishings that he favoured in this, his bedroom, were of Japanese influence. The chintzy floral curtains matched well the black lacquering of his chest of drawers, the dark wood book shelving, the low easy chairs and of course his new futon bed.

That was the reason he slept alone. Although he was married, his wife had been unable to cope with this new addition and preferred the comfort of the four-poster in the guest room. She had not expected her husband to give in to her upon this decision of hers, indeed she had not made it as a threat. Simply, she had grown accustomed to Grumer's fancies, which were more reasoned than the word suggests. And her husband saw no necessity in their sleeping together when that is all they would be doing; sleeping. On the twice weekly occasions when coitus was planned – always the same days unless usurped by a formal engagement – they made love in the guest-room bed. This neither was a change. Grumer did a lot of his work from the bedroom, which doubled up as a study, and didn't want the atmosphere marred by the interference of sex.

Thus, to outside appearances, they were both equally suited by the guidelines which had been set. On the surface, it really did seem that way. Only Grumer was disturbed by the reality of his feelings. Reality which couldn't be suppressed because his desire dictated that it shouldn't be. And this was revealed by his dreams.

It all began one night, a few weeks after his futon bed had been delivered.

The bed was composed of seven layers and it had taken him until that time to get used to sleeping on it. His dreams had been greatly disturbed up to that point. Because, you see, sleeping was hard enough, and dreams only occur in the relaxed state – that of deep sleep.

Aline, his wife, appeared at the threshold of the bedroom. She leant against the door jamb, in one hand holding a thick paperback curled at the corners. Gently, she swayed towards him, watching as he lay propped up in his futon. He wore only boxer shorts in bed and she studied the greying hairs of his chest, moving closer towards him as she did.

Grumer said nothing, he was unused to her entering the bedroom so late at night. She knew that she might be disturbing him as he went over notes taken in his office during the day. And she always knocked before coming in. But it was her expression that surprised him. Her mouth was relaxed into a smile, lip lined and filled in with a deep red. She licked one corner, tucking a stray brown curl behind her ear.

'Dear?' he questioned, wondering with rising anxiety what brought her into his room at this hour, but she held her fingers to her lips, silencing.

Untying the silk dressing-gown that she wore, Grumer was aware of her new silk négligée. He did not speak, but it was

34

neither Sunday morning nor Tuesday evening, and they always met at the top of the stairs close to the guest room. He felt uneasy.

Dropping the gown to her feet, Aline enjoyed her husband's gaze. It was directed at the fullness of her breasts, the nipples hard and visible through the delicate lace of her garment. She lifted the nightdress over her head and he saw that she wore a tight G-string. Laughing, she turned around, displaying the nakedness of her buttocks.

'I always thought horses were elegant.' She spoke watching his reflection in the mirror on the dressing table. He was surveying her carefully. 'They have a tail to cover their cracks.' She continued: 'All you can see is the roundness of the rump and the tail, soft like a curtain.' She turned back to him, her hands feeling for her own backside. 'So appropriate.'

Grumer nodded, sitting up further and waiting for her actions.

Coming towards him, she tore off the G-string, letting it drop to the ground. The curls of her pubic hair were released, only these she had not dyed and they were peppered with grey.

Grumer looked from her pubic hair to her crown, wondering why she allowed this discrepancy. Aline looked after herself diligently; she was aware more than most women of the ageing process. Trainer at a ballet school for thirty years, she had not allowed her body to lose its tautness. Indeed they had a barre installed in the mirrored bathroom, so that she could keep up the suppleness of her body. She enjoyed being able to view her exercises from every direction, checking the extension of her limbs, the hardness of her posture.

Now she straddled him, completely naked, allowing her breasts to move forwards so that their nipples brushed his beard.

Gingerly, Grumer turned her over so that she lay next to him, on her back. He bent over her breasts and held one of her nipples hard, between finger and thumb. He pressed and continued pressing until she called out, reaching for his now erect penis. He pushed her hand away and moved on top of her, burying his head between her thighs. Her skin smelled of the honey creme that she bathed in, but her pudendum was hot and salty. He brushed it hard with his hand, to extricate any loose hairs, before moving in with his tongue and nibbling at her clitoris.

Before he could fully take in his surprise at her actions, at the fact she was allowing him to make love to her in this way, he awoke. Breathing out heavily, he wiped his brow and moved his fingers down to the tear ducts of his eyes, where he brushed out the yellowing corns of sleep.

Pulling at the corners of his duvet, he slid off his futon and hauled himself to his feet. Making his way to his bookshelf, he filed over the spines of the books until he came to the one he was searching for. A book on lucid dreaming.

Once back in bed, tucked up to the chin and with the book balanced on his chest, he began to read. Glancing down the contents list, he turned to the relevant chapter, 'Improving Ability to Control Dreams'.

He had soon realized that part of the dream that he had just had had been controlled by himself. Although he had been asleep, and therefore passive, there was something active in the decisions he had subconsciously made about making love to his wife. It was he who had turned her on to her back, who had forced himself upon her. It was he who had designed the clothes that she wore, he who had determined her actions before they occurred.

Over the ensuing weeks, he learnt how to improve his abilities to begin lucid dreaming; he began by taking time to become aware of his surroundings. Throughout the day, he would pause for moments and take in his position in life. Studying his whereabouts he would repeat to himself his name and the fact that he was awake, in control of the situation. He repeated this ten to fifteen times each day, until one night, in the middle of a dream, the same thing automatically happened.

'I am Dr Ansel Grumer,' he told himself as he discovered the reality of his surroundings despite the fact that he knew that he was asleep. And then he called his wife in his dream and waited for her to appear at the door.

'What is it?' There was faint anger at the root of her voice, she hated being disturbed when she was exercising. 'Come,' and he took her by the hand and led her downstairs.

Still dressed in her black unitard and legwarmers, barefoot, she was thrust by her husband into their Volvo. 'I mustn't wake up, I mustn't wake up,' he challenged himself, aware that any real movement out of the dream state would ruin his chances.

Grumer's heart rate increased as he slid into the driver's seat and switched on the ignition. The tank needed filling, but what the heck, this was a dream, fuel was not a real commodity in relation.

Grumer took his wife to a motel. Charles' Motel, a fifteen-minute drive away. Only because he was dreaming, he was able to skip a lot of the streets, draw himself closer and eliminate traffic lights.

Stopping outside the motel, he drew a key from his blazer pocket, the key to the motel, and unlocking the door, walked right in.

'Hi!' He greeted the member of staff manning the reception

desk, and he invented that he was related to the owner and so an important client who could come and go as he pleased. You see he had the master key to all the bedrooms. He chose the most cramped, dirtiest little room, its walls covered in a peeling textured paper, dark red in colour.

Throwing Aline on to the sagging bed, he peeled off her unitard and legwarmers. She was naked. He was wary of waking up, so he himself did not undress. Suddenly, he was becoming too aware that this was only a dream.

Unzipping his fly, he pulled out his penis and rolled Aline on to her back. Clenching the base of his member, he induced a hard on and felt for the anus between his wife's buttocks. Forcing himself down on her, forcing, forcing, he managed to enter. She struggled, but he focused his mind: he had complete control over her both physically and mentally. Pinning her arms behind her back, he made her cry out in pleasure and arch her long neck upwards. He could only see her hair and he laughed to himself. This way he did not have to acknowledge her existence. Thank God for the ability to render his wife simply a body. He could even metamorphose her physically, change her appearance, turn her into an actress or a beauty queen. Or even the queen!

When he had come, he lay himself flat out on the bed. The mattress was hollowed out where many bodies, different shapes and sizes, had lain.

His wife was still flat on her stomach and in the dim light he could hardly recognize her. Studying her hair, he thought of his patient. The girl who without knowing it had made him come. Catherine, or Maud as she preferred to be called. Catherine Maud Faulkes.

Sighing to himself, he concentrated his energies and

recalled to mind her exact appearance. He tried to change the body of his wife into that of his patient. However, despite this discipline, his powers to control his dreams were not in the advanced state. As he tried to make the subtle change of Aline's hairline into that of Maud's, he awoke. He was however satiated, and the trip had not been completely fruitless.

Over the next few weeks he managed to extend his abilities of lucid dreaming. If he had an argument with his wife, he would turn her into an example of submission before him. For once in his life, all his sexual fantasies were fulfilled, even if he did have to pay the price of awaking to a bed of semen.

The one discrepancy over which he had no control was that of bringing Maud into his dreams; it was almost as if she was aware of what he was doing and was enacting her own personal copy of his dream, but against him. Try as he would, her face would blur as quickly as it had formed, she would not react to his suggestions. The one time he was able to produce her bodily image, she glanced down at his erection and faded from his mind amidst laughter.

Grumer became convinced, however, that this was all part of the hide and seek game of sexual politics. He knew that in reality she would benefit from having closer relations with him and knew that she too was aware of this. The last time that she had consulted with him, he had somehow known that he would see her again and on a personal level. The impossibility of incorporating her into his dream life suggested to him that now was the time for their real relationship to be fulfilled.

When Dr Grumer called her at home, a few days later, this did not come as a surprise to Maud.

She felt, after having spoken to him, that she had willed it to happen. This feeling was accompanied by self-satisfaction, a minor and benign satisfaction that only resulted in her greater sense of security.

The conversation was ambiguous, though Maud felt that she understood the doctor's intentions perfectly.

'Maud, is that you?' The doctor's voice came uneven, slightly embarrassed even, for it must be said he was used to dealing through secretaries. He never put through calls personally; perhaps this was not so much a sign of his priorities as much as a personal dislike of using such a system as the telephone.

'Dr Grumer?' Maud sounded surprised, not as we know unintentionally for she thought that she had been expecting the call. She did not want to disconcert the caller, however, she felt that it was a matter of decorum to preserve his dignity.

'Yes, this is he.' He paused a while before continuing, and Maud felt that she knew what he was going to say before he himself did.

'I've been thinking about our meeting . . .' he continued, clearing his voice.

Maud interjected, 'But you referred me back to my GP.'

'Yes, that's right. Have you seen someone, since then I mean?' he wanted to know.

Dr Grumer was officially retired. He only took on patients privately, and for some reason had been at a loss with Maud's case. He had originally prescribed her the Clomipramine that she hated so much. It made her sweat and she had wondered whether he had chosen that drug on purpose, the way a witch would, in order to inflict such side effects upon her. Perhaps he had felt that it gave him some sort of control over her body, as it of course gave him over her brain. She had given up that drug a long time ago, in favour of something more modern, as her GP had described the Flupenthixol.

'I've been thinking about your case a lot,' the doctor continued, 'and I think I may be able to help you.'

Maud took no time working out in her mind the way she wanted the conversation to go. She would assert her independence, show Dr Grumer that it was a long time since he had had any power over the way her treatment would progress.

'I've an appointment with a doctor at King George's,' she told him, adding, 'with the successor of another retired psychiatrist. This one's much younger, he's taken over all Dr Roper's patients.'

'I see.' Dr Grumer sounded a little disconcerted, in accordance with Maud's intentions.

'Yes, of course the appointment's not for another couple of weeks. I think it's ridiculous how long the waiting time is. I could be dead by then. Half his patients probably arrive on stretchers.' Maud traced the edge of her lower lip with her third finger as she spoke.

Dr Grumer's laughter came a few seconds late and her satisfaction grew. She arched her back a little.

'Well, perhaps I could arrange to see you again, then. Sooner than the next appointment.' His voice lifted a little so that the sentence rose as a question.

'Perhaps,' was Maud's reply.

'However, I'm not really supposed to have anything more to do with your case,' he explained hurriedly, 'so I think it would be best if we kept the meeting between ourselves.'

'A secret, you mean?' Maud asked, smiling.

'Well, you could come to my office, I will inform the secretary of the time and date, only it would be best if you told no one else. I would not want it to cause embarrassment to your new psychiatrist.' He laughed, as if to reassure.

'That's kind of you.' Maud brought formality into her answer, to show that she understood. The two were brought closer together, as if conspiring.

'How about tomorrow, then? Any time.'

'Two o'clock, then,' Maud decided, and she knew that there was relief in Dr Grumer's mind, although he was silent for a moment.

Finally he said, 'I'll expect you.'

Maud put the receiver down, instinctive about the meeting. When she left her first appointment with Grumer, months ago, she had caught him looking at her strangely; at the secretary's desk, she had been organizing the next and last appointment with him and had glanced behind her, sensing nothing. It was the manner in which he had stared at her that had set her thinking. She had felt as if she were an insect, his gaze pinning her with admiration, as if part of a collection. Although she knew that her case must be common, she felt that he was able to understand her. When, after the second appointment, he had advised her admission into the private hospital, she had been surprised that he should think this necessary. She knew that she was not special, she was not even schizophrenic, quite normal really. Then why had he not been able to diagnose her more simply, more readily? She had not thought much about it at the time, had been in too much of a state to do more than concentrate on finding a doctor who could help her. Although now that the drugs had settled her, she could no longer remember how she had formerly been. While taking the medicine prescribed, she felt like a dead leg inside a plaster case. The thick white plaster of Paris encased her wholly, so that although new hairs pushed through the surface of the shaved leg inside, they could not reach the air, breathe and be satisfied.

The leg is a hindrance to the rest of the body, as was Maud's mind to her own. Although she did not think about this, she experienced a dullness mentally and physically, so that she felt separate and isolated from the rest of her world.

The phone call, however, changed everything, Maud had expectations because of the way in which Dr Grumer had approached her. Herr Grumer was how she thought of him, a man usually restricted by his professionalism, now abandoned. For what reason? she asked herself, not wanting to dwell too long on the matter because she trusted her instinct and had long experience of the negative results of relying too heavily on her mind. The mind that was now officially unreliable, advised to be out of use.

When she did not think deeply, Maud felt an extra sense of her own power. She was aware that it was this that had made Grumer call. Grumer was all that he would now be known to her as. Only the surname, as given to schoolboys, particularly of private institutions. His heaviness made her think of a school-boy, the way he had avoided asking too sexual questions, for fear of offending his patient. Maud was very much aware of the psychiatrists' general treatment of the patient. Probing them gently so as not to disturb, knowing that they did not have full control over their reactions. This usually resulted in a patroniz-ing questioning, when Maud would dismiss the doctors' for-mality and laugh off the way they broached their different subjects so tenderly.

Precious. She shuddered at the word, and left it at that. But she liked the discomfort that she could inflict upon herself, and so she deliberately repeated the word to herself, stirred up the connotations that it had for her. She thought back to Geoffrey, a name she disliked. His treatment of her made her feel incestuous. The way he swallowed his coffee, the liquidity of his saliva. His emphasis on sexuality, their closeness in age, rendering her even more uncomfortable at the questions.

She had lied. Almost blushing to herself, she was forced by the side of her that was repellent to the rest. Scowling inwardly, she recalled the way he had phrased his demand for more details.

'Have you had any sexual relations?' he had asked, swallowing with completion as he drew the excess saliva down his gullet.

'Yes.' Maud had drawn the answer from herself, bound to truth.

'When?' he had continued, enforcing that she should pursue herself painfully.

'When I was sixteen. Not since then.'

'Who with?' He made notes as she answered, surely of copious detail. Excessive notes. 'Your boyfriend?'

Maud had nodded.

'How long did the relationship continue?'

'A few months.' Maud's answer was truthful, though at the same time it denied itself the truth. Yes, she had been going out with her boyfriend for several months. But she had slept with him only once. Once. At the end of their relationship, between arguments.

There was a pale frustration in her throat as she withheld desire to elaborate more honestly. So, she had left it at that, not wanting him to acknowledge how brief her sexual experiences were. Of course, since then she had truthfully given details to the same question by an older doctor. But this had not swept away the sense of deceit that she felt. Indeed it made her feel more childish, because it had only been a matter of age that had driven away her honesty on that previous occasion.

She threw these memories to the back of her mind. Angry at her behaviour, angry at the way she made these constant reproaches, instead of siding with herself.

Drawing to the forefront in their place, images of Grumer and 167, Maud pacified herself, conscious of the ebbing of her frustration as when the coolness of milk, washed down, dispels acidity.

It was with careful preparation that Maud readied herself for her meeting with Grumer.

She wished that she had not begun taking drugs; that she had known of their side effects sooner. But she had; and they had discreetly filled out her body so that, although not plump, it was now a larger size altogether. Maud took herself to the bathroom and, divesting herself, pushed down the bath plug and turned on both taps. It was a small bath and filled very quickly. Holding an almost empty bottle of soap creme to the hot tap, she replaced the lid and shook vigorously, emptying it into the gushing water. Checking the profile of her body in the mirror, she was pleased to note that she had begun to lose the weight. If she didn't think about it, but minimized her food intake, it would only take a couple of weeks to regain her figure. This was not a problem, she told herself, for she had no need of her body for that period of time. Smiling slightly, she felt the contours of her breasts with her hands, gauging their present size. They too, had begun to lose their former swelling. Soon she would be free of drugs and could forget the experience completely, one of a series of experiences that made up her life, mostly now dismissed in this manner. Although Maud was able only to plan ahead; she had no present life and no past.

She continually exerted her energies in the hope of creating a future present life. But this was all that it remained; a future present life.

Now, however, things would begin to change; hopefully,

to improve greatly. Maud had awaited the phone call from
Grumer, had since the first time she had met with a psychiatrist
felt that she deserved something in return for the information
that she primed them with. It was a deadening feeling, to meet
with a shrink once or twice, begin to feel an unquestioned
understanding, and then suddenly to be expelled; dismissed
from their knowledge, forgotten to a metal records cabinet,
sacrificed to a manila folder.

Obviously she had more of a hold on Grumer than she
had realized at the time. Their relationship would tip, he was
to become more dependent on her; she could sense it.

Holding her right arm out, Maud sniffed under the armpit.
Not too bad. It was weeks since she had last taken a bath, but
she did shave under her arms regularly. Were the meeting not
to take place that day, she would still have to succumb to the
bathwater. She was beginning to feel clammy all over, knew
that she had about a month's dead skin waiting to be shed.
Previously, she had thought that if she did not wash, a link with
herself was created and maintained. In the same way that people
hesitate before washing after making love when they know they
will not be with that person soon, so Maud knew that the
longer she remained unclean, the more sure she would be about
herself. She would not change, but remain the same person as
she was the day before and the day before that.

Because she had the proof of that, ingrained upon her skin.
Now, as she screwed the taps firmly to a close, she looked
forward to being able to free herself from the past in this way.
Stepping into the water, she shaved her under arms and her
legs, soaped her body and scrubbed the dirt free with a rough
flannel. Over and over her body, a second lather then a third,
scrubbed and repeated, it was not long before the bubbles had

flattened and a scummy grey surface appeared on the bathwater.

When she let the water run out, there was left a line of silty dirt and hairs on the white enamel. This she rinsed away with a cold jet from the shower head.

Untying the chignon of hair piled on to her head, Maud let her head fall forward, shaking it free. She turned on the shower once again, holding the head to the back of her, wetting it thoroughly. The hot water didn't work and soon the jet of cold water left her with a headache. Pouring shampoo on to her palm, she massaged her hands together to create a lather before working this into her hair. Presently, she rinsed the shampoo away, wondering why the bubbling stream flowing towards the bath hole was always greyish, even second time around.

Turning off the supply and squeezing the excess water out of her hair, she grabbed a towel and wrapped it around her head, screwing it tightly so as to trap the wetness in it.

Maud was conscious that she had made no effort with her appearance the last time that she saw Grumer.

She had been wearing the jeans, T-shirt and grey cardigan that made up her present uniform for the last few months. Nor did she want to stray from this pattern today; especially not today, for fear of flattering Grumer, making him think that she had feelings for him that weren't there. A change in costume would imply respect too, as well as perhaps, an improvement in her condition. She wanted him initially to see that she remained the same in spirit from the day of her first meeting with him. That way it would be easier to deceive him with her appearance in the future; the possibilities would be endless. With satisfaction, Maud stepped into her dirty pants and then her jeans, more aware this day of how she had let herself go during her illness. The only concession she made was to wear a bra. It was too long since she had last worn one and vanity made her aware that the effects of going without would be long lasting.

Unwinding the towel from her hair, she pulled the white T-shirt over her head, thrusting her body forward so that the drops would trickle on to the floor and not down her back. Although fairly long, Maud managed to dry her hair quickly, rubbing it vigorously between the towel, turning the towel round when that side was saturated.

The trainers that she had been wearing, also for the last few months, were beginning to exude a mouldy humidity, even when they were on her feet. Still, this did not deter her, anxious that she should be correctly presented in every way; she was very much conscious of the psychiatrists' obsession with analysis and felt that her deception, however minimal, could be a personal triumph.

Thus would end the relationship between patient and doctor; to be, in her eyes, corrected. No longer would she experience that sense of loss when the doctor's temporary interest in her faded. Indeed she would be sure to have the inherently fickle attitude of the psychiatrist made an example of. This would be one of the main aims of her plan.

The Loden coat that she wore was the last reminder of the year she had spent at a girls' boarding school when she was seventeen. It had formed part of her uniform and she still wore it to make up for the expense she had caused by leaving school prematurely to take her A-levels. It was too costly an item to abandon as she had the rest of the uniform. She felt now, having spent her last few months wearing it, that it was her trademark. Only continental business men and elderly ladies wore Loden coats around Chelsea. Maud wondered whether people had begun to notice her more since she had taken to wearing the same clothes, day in, day out.

Shrugging off this idea, she thrust a few of her belongings into the coat pocket and left the house, locking the front door securely.

The King's Road was fairly busy. It was lunch-time and there was a preponderance of schoolgirls and shoppers, all, she noted, walking far too slowly. Living near the King's Road, Maud was tired of the perpetually slow filter of people down this main street. There was no one of purpose to be seen and she quickened her pace, threading through the steadfast groups.

At Sloane Square tube station, she queued to buy her ticket from the attendant in the small office. She needed to change a five-pound note and although the machines had been made to accept these notes, when she fed hers into the machine, it had, as on all previous occasions, been rejected.

Once through the barrier, Maud stepped quickly down the staircase that led to the southbound Circle and District lines. The train was not long in coming. A cooling breeze down the tunnel heralded its arrival. As it eased itself to a standstill, the doors opened and the crowded carriage nearest her was emptied, its heat dissipated. Maud stepped in and leaned against the glass panel close to the doors. The train moved on, speeding up until it rattled through the long cabled tunnel that led to the platform at Victoria. As soon as the button lit up, hissing, Maud released the doors and freed herself from the carriage. She was walking down the edge of the platform towards the Victoria line and she watched for the train to leave, so that there were only a few inches between herself and the gap for the rails. Down the stairs and then across to the escalator; Maud stepped on and her section lowered into a step bearing her downwards. Turning left as her escalator stair faded under the floor, she waited on the northbound platform for the train that would take her the three stops to Oxford Circus. It was not long in coming and she took her eyes off the gallery poster that she had been studying in order to hop on. This time the carriage was almost vacant, and she sat down in a seat reserved for the elderly and disabled. Raising her eyes, she traced the Victoria line map that bordered the top of the carriage.

Then across to the rows of advertisements on either side. Maud had an aversion to train carriages. She disliked the way people wore a set facial expression, shunning all eyes. She felt that there was nowhere that she was free to look, even when there were only a few passengers, as now. Only a handful of people got on and got off at Green Park, and then the train arrived at Oxford Circus. It was an older model, and the doors opened automatically and not selectively. Maud stepped off and made towards the WAY OUT sign. Up the escalator and then up the few steps before exiting through the ticket barrier, where-upon she was greeted by the Oxford Street breeze. Reading the signs above, she chose the Regent Street/Oxford Street opening to the station and was soon at street level. On her way out there was a small kiosk and a newspaper stand. The first edition of that day's *Evening Standard* was selling and she bought a copy. Unfolding the paper she gazed absently at the headlines before folding it twice and fitting it under her arm. Her dentist was also in Harley Street and she knew that route by heart, although not until she was faced with the different possibilities of roads to cross and streets to follow. When soon enough she reached the end of Harley Street she was looking for, she found the correct door and stepped up, pausing to collect her thoughts. There was a button marked PATIENTS, and it was this that she pressed. Presently, the speaker emitted a dull buzzing noise, a sign for Maud to push the door open. Inside, she passed the main reception, informing them of her appointment. Fourth floor, was the reply and she pressed for the lift. There was a long wait as the old-fashioned lift drew itself down the shaft to the ground level.

Sliding back the metal gate, she was soon inside, checking her appearance in the half-length mirror at the back. Carefully making her selection from the lit panel of buttons, there was a faint whirr as the metal ropes strained, drawing the lift upwards. Above the door, a sign lit up as each floor passed by ... 1 ... 2 ... 3 ... and the lift shuddered to a halt, bouncing minimally. By the time Maud had reached the front door of the building, she had begun to feel a fluttering pain in her lower stomach. As the lift rose, the pain shifted achingly to her bowels and she clenched her buttocks instinctively. Now, she waited as the doors parted, checking her appearance once more before stepping out of the lift and walking down the corridor to Grumer's office. She passed his secretary's desk on the way, but the high swivel chair was empty. Surprising at such a busy time of the afternoon; Maud wondered whether this had been planned. Glancing over the desk at the leather-bound appointment book that lay open, she saw that her name had been entered in the box marked 2.30 p.m. to 3.30 p.m.

Her fist pausing as she reached Grumer's door, she finally knocked. The sound of her knuckles was one of quiet urgency, three quick knocks, questioning.

'Come in.' Maud had been waiting to hear Grumer's voice, wondering if, then, her memory of it would return. This assumption was correct, she recalled the foreign nasal quality and the way the vowels were lightly stressed.

When she pushed open the door, it was to see the psychiatrist sitting upright at his desk.

His hands were clasped together on his knees and he moved them towards his desk, shuffling and rearranging papers.

Maud smiled. 'Dr Grumer,' she acknowledged before indicating the seat opposite him with her eyes.

'Yes. Do sit down,' he encouraged, his lips curled at the corners in an embarrassed fashion.

Maud had not expected him to be so restrained in his manner. When she had visited him more formally as his patient, he had adopted a welcoming front, putting her immediately at ease if a little too politely. Now he simply stared at her, taking the whole of her in, although he was careful for his eyes not to stray. He did not want to appear covetous.

'I see your secretary isn't here today.' There was no trace of suspicion in her voice although Maud had to concentrate so as not to betray her personal feelings.

'Ah, Alison took a late lunch today,' Grumer answered, not uncomfortably. 'She has an appointment of her own this afternoon.'

Maud nodded, pausing before asking, 'So, what exactly did you want to see me about?' Already in her mind, her plan was beginning to fashion itself, to join together all her ideas. Perhaps she would be able to exorcize her feelings, all the resentment that she secretly harboured for the psychiatrists. Collectively. She could use 167 in so doing, creating a double satisfaction. If she could somehow bring in this most important symbol, one so pertinent to herself as 167 was, and if she could withhold her feelings about it from Grumer, while including him at the same time, then perhaps she would benefit most fully from her plan.

Grumer was a long time in answering, she wondered in

53

fact if he had made notes, for he concentrated his eyes on his desk, at the papers in front of him. Of course, she remembered, all doctors had files on each of their patients. She did not, however, think it was right for Grumer to use this against her, particularly since they had contrived this meeting together, despite others. She did not try to quell her internal anger, indeed she savoured it while keeping it away from Grumer, out of her features, her mannerisms.

'I think . . .' He finally spoke, looking up and clasping his hands together again, a habit that Maud remembered from her previous knowledge of him. 'Yes, I am quite sure, that you would benefit from having a stronger relationship with a psychiatrist.'

Maud raised one eyebrow suggestively, wanting him to explain his motives, make himself open to her.

'Of course, from what you have told me, I am sure that the psychiatrist at King George's will attempt to build a trust between you. This is an accepted practice,' he assured, 'and one that is very necessary if the patient is to benefit most completely.'

Maud nodded, not quite sure of her response, withholding it temporarily.

'In your case however,' again Grumer glanced down at his notes, 'I think that this is going to be more difficult than usual. You are a writer, and from my previous experience with you I became aware of the importance that you place on human nature.'

At this point Grumer pulled himself away from his desk and stood up. He paced over to the front of the desk and half stood, leaning his bottom and his left leg for support against its edge. From here, he spoke to her more directly, his eyes maintaining contact with hers. 'Usually such a relationship between doctor and patient is false; although the patient is not conscious of this. The psychiatrist builds up their confidence in him, urges them to be completely truthful and this allows that there is trust involved. But there is a frankness lacking. In his turn, the psychiatrist is not completely honest, he knows that he is not on the same level as the patient. How can he be?' Here Grumer laughed; an attempt, as Maud saw it, to placate. 'The answer is that he is to his patient more a parent than a colleague, a close associate. I'm sure that you are aware that the psychiatrist's response is always limited. It is not for him to criticize, or even to hold an opinion . . .'

Maud sighed angrily. 'And the patient has got to accept all of this, get used to the way they're treated, learn to trust the shrink. And then what? Referred to another doctor, prescribed some pills. That's the last they see of them.'

Grumer nodded slowly. 'That is usually the case. What do you think would happen if an attempt were made at a more durable relationship?' He got up and walked across the room where he straightened a framed Millais print. 'It wouldn't even be right.'

Maud shook her head. She was beginning to think that the whole appointment had been a waste of time. How was she to instil into this man her beliefs? He was too arrogant of his own knowledge; a self knowledge. Maud couldn't stand those who were unable to accept that others did not think like them. Surely if you had a point of view, it was obvious that others' would be different. Should be allowed to be. She glanced to her left, where, as on her previous visits, was a long glass case. Inside there was a pike, glazed like artificial bread. 'Is the fish real?' she asked.

'What?' Grumer turned round, his fingers bristling at his beard.

'The fish,' she pointed to the wall, 'real?'

'Oh, yes,' came his distracted answer. 'Look, let's be honest.' Returning to his desk, he sat down, opening the drawer and shuffling among its contents. Extracting a spring-loaded cigarette case, the lid opened to the slight pressure of his thumb and he brought the case up to his nose. Taking one of the cigarettes, he drew himself down to desk level and lit it at the heavy crystal lighter, puffing contentedly.

'I understand you better than you think.' His voice challenged; he did not smile but seemed to study her face for response.

Maud realized that on her last two visits to Grumer she had focused on the preserved pike in order to concentrate herself away from particularly testing questions. She forced her eyes off the scratched glass front, relaxing her body, suddenly powerful.

'I know what you're saying,' was her indication to Grumer that he had been right, that he rightfully acknowledged the game that they had been playing. It was a game that all psychiatrists played with Maud. Or at least that was her interpretation. The game stank. Bluntly or subtly, most indirectly, whichever the approach, there was one target, one plastic aim. Reduce the patient to the stage where they asked, pleaded, for help. Question them first formally, try to break down the barriers, prod at their personal terror and make them admit it. They couldn't cope on their own. Needed your help, needed you. It was the same game the prostitute played. Revenge against man, against the whole of the male species' love of control. Find their weakness and send them flying, either by sex or by careful psychological plying. Unfair advantage and all that.

'Have you ever had the whole truth given to you, bathed in it, not secretly but with the patient?'

Grumer shook his head, without emotion. At this point he could not afford emotion.

Maud knew that she was for the moment in control. She also knew that Grumer had personal standards. If she was fair to him now, he could only but return this treatment later on. It wasn't a question of trust, simply the psychiatric code of ethics. As seen by Maud.

'When I tell you what it all boils down to, you'll laugh.' She grinned, the situation lightening. Grumer rocked gently backwards in the synthetic leather swivel chair. Then he swung round slowly, propelled by the gently balletic movements of his feet, and round again.

'I've got to retain your interest, you can't expect me to tell you everything at once.'

Grumer stopped, facing his desk once more. He cocked his head. 'You see, I could tell you; it's not that I don't want to. But it wouldn't be explaining everything properly.' There was anxiety in Maud's voice and Grumer indicated with his hands for her to quieten.

'It's not like a book,' she continued, 'no question of just summarizing the plot, giving you a character list and explanatory notes of their relationships. Besides, you do want to enter into it.' She spoke these words carefully, joyfully and with intrigue.

Only a few nights before, Maud had had a dream that she felt was significant to her. It was of a man she had met at a gathering. An old friend of her parents, an artist. He was not very tall, with roughened skin like the peel of a citrus fruit. His hair was dark, though unkempt and with grey showing beneath. Although he was English, his origins could not have been less so. And, in the next room, she had taken his hand and he had stood silently and unresponsive.

'You must wash, though,' she had heard herself saying. 'I want you to smell of soap.' And even now she could recall the faintly rancid smell of his clothes, the turpentine that was the only cleaning fluid that his fingers knew.

It had been odd, because there was no conversation between the two, and Maud knew that this artist was merely an extension of herself. The personification of how she wanted her plans to go, an example of her control.

Although proof perhaps of an impalpable narcissism, there was no way that this dream life could be transferred to reality. Maud was never attracted to people that she knew. Grumer was to take the artist's place, but she would be careful never to touch him. She must behave in a manner that was decorous, if only so that he should not be able to come near her, and to feel right in doing so. There must be a physical barrier, though she knew at times she would have to be cruel to enforce it.

'I can't begin now, there are places that I'll have to take you. And part of it's a riddle anyway. Though it is true.' She spoke as Grumer frowned.

'When then?' was all that he asked.

'Sometime next week. It starts with a showing at the cinema, of *Last Tango in Paris*, I guess that's all you have to know.'

'Significant enough on its own,' was his reply.

'Yes, but don't get it out on video. It's always on at some screen. I'll organize the tickets and then call you.'

Grumer leant forward. 'But there's no sex involved. I know that there can't be.' He was puzzled, recalling the records that he had been over with Dr Bilsen. She had had sex only once, he was sure of that.

Maud nodded, saving further explanation. She was aware of what he was thinking. She thought that by now she had a fair idea of his mind processes.

Maud got up. She did not want him to show her out, but went to the door, opening it and peering out. 'Your secretary's not back.' Looking at him, she smiled. Not a real smile, more of a curling of her lips' edges. Grumer turned round in his chair a little, so that he faced her.

Maud turned round. Pulling her arms across the front of her body, and diagonally on to her sides, she began to shiver lightly, feeling with her hands the contour of her hips. From where Grumer sat, it appeared that the hands did not belong to Maud, but there was someone facing her, running their hands over her instead.

'Have you seen this?' Maud asked, shimmying a while longer. She turned round abruptly, but he had checked his expression. Non-committal as always. 'Well, I'll call you, OK.' He nodded and she left the room, closing the door behind her.

Moving quietly over the carpeted floor, and across to the lift at the end of the corridor, she pressed the CALL button. It lit up to a red square and the lift could be heard, surging upwards, spurred on by a whirring of ropes. The pulley needed oiling. Every few seconds it would crank and jar just a little as it turned. Bouncing to a halt, the lift doors opened, and Maud was ferried downwards. In the fewest of movements she had made it to the door, and was then free of the building. She could feel her pupils contract as they got used to the sunlight.

The control that Maud felt as she left Grumer's office was not usual and much preferable to the emptiness and sense of violation that she was more used to. She wondered what sort of emotion she had left him with. Perhaps he was immune to uncontrolled feelings. Definitely, he had not displayed any thoughts about their meeting earlier. She had been aware that he had been deeply impressed by her somehow, it was only the nature of this impression that she had no insight into.

Maud knew that by reliving the past with Grumer, she would be at the same time protecting herself from him. It was obvious that as she slipped back into her previous relationships and experiences, albeit through only her imagination and recognition, so she would move further and further away from him. The more detail that she added, the more information that she imparted, the less contact he would be allowed. She wondered how he would react to this reality. Perhaps, unlike on any previous occasions, he would make an attempt to follow her to have himself brought in to her past. Of course, that would not be possible, even for her to accomplish and she would be the one in control, this time. But it would be interesting to observe his reactions, to watch as she distanced herself from him.

Grumer, in his office, had not moved from his seat. No longer did he stir in his chair. He was quite still, concentrating as he relived the interview that had just occurred. Drawing the manila folder from the drawer in the right side of his desk, he opened it flat in front of him. Watching. He felt that somehow, with all this knowledge of Maud, the factual account of her life, relationships with parents, her own words, he would be able to piece an understanding of her together.

He closed the folder, sure that part of Maud's plan was the waiting. There was nothing that he could do until he next heard from her and even then he would not be warned of what to expect. *Last Tango in Paris*, that had only been the clue.

Perhaps it was not even a clue, relevant, yes, but only in the light of what she would soon tell him. He was sure that she had enjoyed immensely the idea of him toying with her every word, wasting his time with recollections of her responses and revelations.

He had been given the minimum information, however. And she had promised that she would let him into the most intimate aspect of her life. The underlying reality at which he had been guessing during their two previous meetings. He was not new to the business. And very much aware that the patient's main priority was to keep for themselves that which remained most important to them. At the same time, however, they would always make a conscious effort to give enough information, or so they thought, to enable themselves to be helped. It was seldom enough, though, and as meetings progressed, so this reality became increasingly important, both to psychiatrist and patient. A battle loomed between them, and it was from this that ensued the failure of real understanding. Because this sort of understanding was not desirable. The psychiatrist was, after all, the enemy. And so the two parties would begin to resent each other, the patient when they slipped into themselves, unaided, and the psychiatrist if, finally, the patient committed suicide. That, of course, was the final insult.

Maud's first attendance at the King George III Hospital occurred soon after this meeting of hers with Grumer.

Although she hoped that it would be with his aid that she finally recovered, she did not want to isolate herself from orthodox treatment. This was not something that she felt that she could afford to do. The King George III Hospital was in Kensington and so she walked there on the morning of her appointment. The building was old and of a traditional architecture; this much was emphasized by its situation adjacent to the heavily shaped Cromwell Hospital with its turquoise windows and oblong structure.

The George III comprised a main frame of older buildings with more modern additions out of sight around the back. There was no main entrance, patients and visitors were directed by a series of signposted routes. It took Maud a good fifteen minutes before she found the Mental Health Unit, the door to which was marked for hearing aid repairs.

The surround of the reception desk was an old wooden frame, much like a picture frame. It had been poorly thrown together and served no real use since Maud had to bend and thrust her head through the gap to speak to the man on duty.

'I've an appointment at eleven,' she informed him.

'What's your name?'

'Maud Faulkes,' she replied, glancing to the wall clock. It was almost eleven now and she did not expect the long wait that was to follow.

'If you go round to the waiting room, you'll be called for your appointment,' she was told. Following these instructions, she turned right and into a spacious room that led to a smaller sunlit one where coffee was served.

Seating herself at one of the three round tables carefully laid out with a patchwork of pulp magazines, Maud looked round. There was no one else in this main part of the room. There were voices coming from the coffee bar and presently a man wearing a purple shirt and tight purple trousers walked into the section where she was sitting. The trousers were thick and woolly, and the weave was composed of wide stripes. Maud stared at the back of the man's neck. His skin was thick and she could make out the faint growth of new hair that tailed off from his scalp. The man, black, had his Afro hair shorn close to his head and she concentrated on the beads of perspiration that hung to the hairs on his nape.

He turned and, ignoring her, returned to his seat next door. The chairs and tables in there were of white wrought-iron, Victorian in style. A radio was playing and a heavily built woman sang along to 'My Girl'. All that Maud could see of her was her long thick legs, clad in black leggings. She wore sandals and Maud saw the pale soles of her feet as she tapped in time to the music.

A woman appeared in the doorway.

'Maud?' she called and Maud got up and followed her out of the room, expressionless. She thought of the two in the next room listening to music, of their acceptance of the hospital. They were obviously patients though perhaps attending the day centre. She was unsure.

'My name's Alice.' The woman turned to her, smiling as she pushed open the door to a very small room like a box, barely furnished. Another woman was already seated there and she looked up as they entered.

'Sit down,' came the invitation, and Maud sank down on the hard school seat.

'This is Jenny, she's the social worker and will be attending all your appointments at King George's—' dropping the rest of the title.

Jenny smiled. 'Hello, Maud.'

'Hello.' Inertia reigned; she shifted in her seat, uncomfortable at the proximity between herself and the other two women. They sat diagonally opposite her, so that she was almost in the middle, unsure of where to fix her eyes.

At first the questions were routine, ones that she had been asked countless times. Full names, dates, family particulars. Maud listened to her voice as she gave the answers. She was completely aware of how the two hung on every word that she spoke. She was a focal point, homed in on, subject of their gaze.

As she spoke, she was amused at the dead quality of her voice. There was none of its nasal quality that she was so used to hearing, reverberating inside her head. She found the sound of her voice comforting, it seemed to direct itself inwards.

She attempted to articulate, to throw her voice further away. Aware that she was probably a boring subject, she began to elaborate on answers that normally would have been glossed over.

Did she think that people in the street knew what she was thinking?

No. But she used to years ago.

How long ago?

Oh, she wasn't sure, four or five years perhaps.

Were there ever voices inside her head, telling her to do things?

It's difficult to distinguish between your own voice disguised and independent ones.

Did she believe that things she read or heard were of special significance to her?

Elaborate.

Was the television talking to her directly?

No.

Perhaps, though, her thoughts were transmitted to the world via the television?

No!

Were there ever thoughts, implanted in her mind, that she could not control?

Yes.

What thoughts?

To steal, to hurt people, to prostitute.

For how long?

The last couple of years.

Did the social worker have any questions to ask Maud?

Yes. She turned to face Maud, her face of frank directness.

'Maud.'

'Yes.' Maud looked up at her, returning the trust, though humorously.

'I'd like to just ask, how long have you been feeling that you generally couldn't cope – the way that you were going?'

'About eighteen months.'

'I see.' She nodded to emphasize her ability to empathize with Maud. She cared, you see. And she probably did. Only Maud was sick of her puke-ridden understanding. There was a gulping enthusiasm to help in the openness of her features. Maud could imagine her at university; could see how she would have fitted in to the hall corridor. Plain, well liked but not often considered. Just there, part of the corridor of students. Maud noticed, though, that her teeth were very white. Neat, strong, pearly teeth. No, that didn't quite go – they should have been yellow. Maud's teeth were creamy coloured. They had been yellowing when she smoked, but it was now a year since she had given up. And she liked her large straight English teeth, creamy so that when she wore lip gloss there was a naturalness. Her face was real because it was composed of colours and textures that existed in nature although perhaps dismissed in life for the more sterilized browns and whites.

Vaginal discharge had no place in the English language. Women's bodies were as functionless as Barbie dolls. That is, they gave pleasure, could induce orgasms, but were clean and their pubic hair never grew, or worse still curled off on to underwear or into plug holes.

If Maud found the social worker's presence that day to be an affront, she could not believe it when the woman's intrusiveness extended itself to the following day when she was allocated an appointment with Dr Nixon, the consultant psychiatrist.

Because he was the successor to the last doctor that she had seen, she hoped that he would be pleasant looking, in order that she may be allowed some distraction from the meeting's sense of routine.

She did not expect that that day it would be Jenny who, smiling, collected her from the waiting room. The psychiatrist's room was very pleasant. It was unlike the rest of the hospital's run-down appearance and had been tastefully thrown together. There was actually a theme to the decor. Low pale sofas and a clear glass table that ran its length.

Maud thought of nothing as she sank into the colourless upholstery, Jenny beside her, upright and benign.

She held a clipboard to her chest and sat posed, ready for the doctor to take over, her face a show of her willingness. Not seeking approval as much as knowing that she was approved of. The doctor came forward, tall and of medium build; his white coat seemed very much a part of him, as though perhaps it lent him his abilities. His brain could have been a microchip in the small breast pocket, but wired up to his head so that his facial expressions seemed an immediate front to his energy.

His eyes were small and round; they were screwed into his head so that they focused strongly and with difficulty on Maud.

'You've met Jenny?' he asked her, summoning his voice upwards from the embedded cords in his throat. Although he was a large man, there was almost no sound, he was rendered weak, the chip had failed.

'Yes, we met yesterday,' Maud replied and they looked at

each other, Jenny smiling as she tilted her head to the left, Maud pushing herself deeper into her body for protection. Her ability to do this had risen from the great series of such meetings that she had experienced. She could answer the most intimate questions with ease by drawing her soul within and letting her brain rule her. Although the brain implies the soul, it only functions directly on its own. That is to say that answers can be hunted but that no consideration can be made. The sense of the individual will not be apparent, and it is that after all that the psychiatrist must tap into. Feeling the patient recoil all the while.

When Dr Nixon paused between questions to think, his eyes went up inside his head and he held his mouth open slightly, pushing the top lip outwards. He sucked in air almost noiselessly as he did so, his hands together, the first fingers at a triangular point.

'Do you think . . .' The question was directed intensely at Maud, so that her eyes connected with his hypnotically. She shuddered inside herself.

'Do you think that your problems are an internal thing or caused by external effects?' He was pleased at his question and Maud wondered whether he ran it past all his clients. Is that what they did, these psychiatrists? She turned round impulsively as if to check for an autocue.

'Internal.' She nodded as she replied and so did he, so that he seemed to catch her and hold her mind for a second with his. Inwardly she cringed at the closeness that she could sense he was trying to develop. A closeness that encompassed Jenny who was proud that she was allowed to sit in at these interviews. Jenny the shepherdess.

'I think so,' was his response, 'that's definitely what my

answer was to have been. It's something internal.' Job satisfaction here, heightened by Jenny's appraisal.

Then he outlined how he would like to approach Maud's case; there were several steps that could be taken – she could be referred to the Psychology Department for a more detailed assessment, and she could also attend a day centre.

He now asked the questions. 'Would you agree to see the team in the psychology department?'

'Yes,' Maud answered.

He took up again. 'And will you attend the day centre here in the Mental Health Unit?'

'No,' was her answer.

He nodded all the while. 'Right, well I'll get on to that, then.' He breathed inwards. 'And now for the ponderous question.' Pausing as he caught her look, 'Will you promise me that you won't commit suicide?' he asked.

'Yes,' Maud hurried past her answer, embarrassed, more grossly so than by any question she had ever been asked. The cloying intimacy of the situation coupled with the voyeurism of the social worker set her body in the escape mode. She felt her muscles clench as she held her breath, pushing time past her, dying for her release from the office. She was sure that when they all left, the room would be temporarily marked by their combined smells. This thought sickened her.

'Will you destroy all your pills?' he continued, unaware of her discomfort.

She nodded curtly and felt the saliva curdle at the back of her throat at his following words. 'I know that it has been hard for you in the past few weeks not to commit suicide' – there was gravity in his voice, though he restrained any awe – 'and that you have had a real struggle. And I respect the fact that you haven't killed yourself.'

What was she to say?

Silently, out of the corner of her eye, she could see Jenny, now turned very much towards her and nodding obviously at the doctor's words. She felt the two of them cave in on her and retreated further from the situation.

'If you feel between now and your next appointment that you need some help,' he now explained, 'call the hospital and they'll put you in touch with either myself or one of the other doctors on duty.'

'I'll be fine,' Maud reassured him.

'Even so, keep it in mind.'

'I will, but I shan't need to trouble anyone.'

'It's important that you do. I feel that it would be a tragedy if you committed suicide,' he let her know.

'Right,' she answered, all three of them now moving to the door.

'Jenny will show you out,' Dr Nixon said, holding out his hand.

She took it, feeling the coolness of his skin against her humid fingers.

'Thank you,' were her words as she left the room, followed by the social worker.

'How did you like Dr Nixon?' Jenny turned to Maud in the corridor, lightening the situation.

'Oh, he's very nice.' Maud had felt sympathetic towards the doctor, although she thought that he was strange. Though he was quite young, the skin beneath his small eyes dragged in ruched semi-circles. She wondered what he was really like, what his personal life was like.

'Mmm,' Jenny agreed with her, 'he was very understanding I thought,' and Maud nodded at this, looking onwards silently. As they reached the reception desk, they paused and Jenny continued, 'Do you feel better now that you've talked with him?'

'I suppose so.' Maud felt increasingly uncomfortable at this interrogation. She wished that there was some way that she could reassure Jenny that she would be fine if let alone.

'Good.' Her voice was optimistic. 'Now, I'll give you my number and whenever you feel you need to talk to someone, call me.' She leant through the wooden frame to talk to the receptionist, a fine-featured black man who seemed out of place in the hospital. There did not seem to be enough energy for him, behind the wooden frame; the job seemed too constricted.

He handed her a square of paper and a biro and she leant forwards to the edge of the reception desk to write.

Her hand was rounded and the letters carefully formed. She seemed to be making it obvious with the care that she took that she had time for Maud, who sighed. She was beginning to feel fussed, wanted to be left alone, had tired of the antiseptic atmosphere of King George's.

Jenny handed her the paper and she stared at the letters and digits, without assimilating any of them. She had forgotten for the moment how to read, to see the symbols in relation to one another.

'Now, the first number's the one that I'm usually at,' came the patient explanation, intent on her understanding, 'and if there's no answer, then call the second number. The people there will always know where to find me. And,' she added, 'as Dr Nixon said, you can always call the reception number and they'll put you through to a doctor.'

'Thanks, I'll keep that in mind,' Maud assured her, completely sure that she would never need to contact the social worker. She thought to herself that she would rather kill herself than call Jenny, that this was simply an inducement to suicide. Feeling the corners of her mouth tighten into a smile, she relaxed the muscles at once, concentrating on the white paper. 'Thanks for your help,' she quickened their parting with.

'I'll see you very soon,' Maud was guaranteed, and she made her way to the door, pulled to the air outside as if it were a pole and herself a magnetic strip.

Outside, the two nurses who she had seen on her way in were still sitting chatting. They sat on a bench, uniform dresses pulled over their crossed knees, in the small triangle of garden. There were two flower-beds separated by York paving, the soil poorly turned, Maud could see from where she stood.

The one nearest to her looked up as she passed and remained silent until she was far away from them.

As she walked home, she concentrated on the visual, not wanting to allow her mind to churn over the morning's events. She was indignant at the social worker's presence at her meeting with the psychiatrist. She wished that she could say something, make her feelings known. At the same time, however, she felt that this attitude would be interpreted as presumptuous. It was as if her silence indicated the appreciation that she knew was deemed necessary by the hospital staff. She was lucky enough to have people helping her. That's what they would think. Maud knew that when she was in this environment, being treated by the hospital doctors, she would have to cut off that part of her that concerned itself with the way things appeared, the rights and wrongs. She was very much aware of her abilities of analysis, shrewdness and perception. It was these that had resulted in the argument with the doctor in Bristol. She had learned to play dumb, was sure of how others wished her to behave. If she did not accept this, she would never make it through the lengthy NHS process that would lead to a diagnosis and recovery. That is why she had a special attitude tailored to the way patients were perceived in such conditions. She became only that part of her that lived actively, and was aware of the irony of this. For, deeply, she knew that her problem lay in her ability to live in the present and thus she would be stunted. Still, by relying on this part of her nature, her shortcomings would be made obvious and this was how she would be best understood.

At the time of the meeting she had thought the idea of her contacting the hospital before her next appointment ludicrous. The suggestion gave off the uncomfortable intimacy which she most detested. However, although she heard from the Psychology Department within the next few days, she learned that her appointment for the assessment was not for two weeks. They had sent her a lengthy questionnaire to aid them in their decision regarding her treatment. When Maud read the questions, she felt herself unable to concentrate frankly on the aspects of herself that the requirement of knowledge was for.

She had to describe in detail a recent dream that she had had, to recount a childhood experience that had been impressionable. She could not force herself to impart such knowledge, especially on paper. It was not as if she was communicating with anyone and she felt that the attempts were completely one-sided. They would never know her responses for, indeed, they were her responses.

She sent off the half-filled questionnaire that had incited her to anger.

The frustration that she was left with was of the gnawing kind, not strong enough to have any effect, but which was too intrusive to be shrugged off. It transformed itself into anger.

Anger at the social worker, at the psychiatrist, and now at those who had anonymously made themselves known to her through the series of questions that she had been sent.

Despite all these feelings, it was not long before her thoughts began once again to pile on top of each other. She was hounded by the pressure of these thoughts, but they did not even express themselves in her mind. They merely hung there, inadmissible.

How did they manifest themselves in her mind? Not so much actively as by prevention. They made her thoughts obsessive, whirring continuously through her brain, preoccupying her. She was unable to concentrate on the external, although this handicap did not seem to stem from herself.

And presently she began to express these compiled emotions physically.

On waking, there would be occasions when she was forced lividly out of bed; would jump up the second that her mind began to cease focusing on whatever dream it was that occupied her. She would not have reached reality before finding herself upright, palpitating, rigid.

This immediate panic would work itself up throughout the day until she was unable to concentrate on anything; not even her misery. At such times, thoughts of suicide did not concern themselves with the idea of cessation of life; simply she needed a fast way out from her discomfort. This was what the bottle of pills settled on the top of the fridge offered.

Standing against the fridge door, eyes level with the bottle of pills, she would consider the effects longingly; only she was too aware of the probabilities of such an overdose – too many and she would simply vomit them out, not enough and she would wake all too easily or find herself damaged mentally. She was also fairly knowledgeable about the varying strengths of pharmaceuticals. The pills that she at present considered were Flupenthixol. Their strength was only 0.1 mg. Amitriptyline capsules, on the other hand, were 25 mg in strength. How was she to know which would be more lethal, especially when the two anti–depressants were of different types, acting on the brain in incomparable ways?

Hysteria, when it reached her, engulfed her body totally. She became convulsive, crying and gasping, unsure of how she was to continue; the idea of the passage of time was, to her, unbelievable. And if believable, then surely unacceptable. More minutes such as these that she could not cope with and hours of minutes, and days of hours of minutes too. Shrinking into a corner next to the wardrobe in her room, she clung to a PVC carrier bag that swung from its handle, a Harrods' bag. Maud could feel the distortions that her facial muscles made, involuntarily. The redness of her skin was transposed in her innerness as heat, great gashes of heat across her eyes and cheeks.

The pores of her skin were angry, scabby and slimy with tears. Holding her hand to her mouth, she gnawed at her nails for comfort and then threw herself upright once more. Pacing the length of the room, what to do, what to do, a solution had to be found, if only she had the courage to take the pills. Only she felt that there was so much that she must complete before death; books that she needed to write, her dog that was her responsibility to look after – how trivial it seemed, but it was a duty and if skimped, would make her ache with dissatisfaction.

Finally, she conceded to call the hospital. Why, she knew not, only she did not know of any alternative. She wanted her brain zoinked out of her body, a grand shock to bounce her marbles and set free their thoughts.

Creeping upstairs, she grabbed the telephone receiver. The

number she knew by heart and she dialled with rapid movements. Pause as the connection was made, as the phone rang
at the other end, as she waited for it to be picked up.

'King George's.' The voice was dull and muffled.

'Hello.' Maud had not planned what she was going to say,
though the words did not seem to be coming from herself; 'I'm
a patient of Dr Nixon. He told me to call the hospital if ever
I was feeling unwell.'

'Right. And what's your name?'

'Maud Faulkes,' she replied, appeased just by having made
the call.

She curled up in the leather chair, putting her thumb to
her teeth, sucking.

'Right, and what's the matter. How are you feeling, then?'

'Depressed.'

'Has anything brought it on?'

'No. Just comes and goes.'

'Have you been thinking about killing yourself?'

'Yes.'

A pause, then the voice softened, 'How?'

'I've got pills.'

'Didn't the doctor ask you to destroy them?'

'Yes, but my parents manufacture drugs, so there didn't
seem to be any point. They're always at hand.'

'Hmm. Would you like to come down to the hospital?'

'No. I don't think it's necessary.'

'Well, if you're thinking of hurting yourself.'

Maud shrank back. 'Oh, I'll be all right.' Her throat tight-
ened as she felt herself let the opportunity slip from between
her fingers. She felt a stab at herself that she had deliberately
let it slip.

'You see, I don't know how ill you are. I've never met you.

If you'd like to come down now and talk to me . . .'

Maud savoured the reassurance of the voice, wanting it to belong solely to her. This angered her. It was the psychiatrist's ruse. Give all of yourself to the patient, but to each patient. Never to let yourself belong specially to any one patient. It was all a lie. To make them feel temporarily protected, closer than by any parent.

'No. I'm OK. I think I'd better go now.'

'Are you sure?'

'Yep, 'bye,' and she put the phone down, heavy inside herself because of the self-denial that she had caused. She did not understand why she had done it. It was as if she needed the help, but had too much pride not to manage on her own.

Savouring the conversation, she let herself reel off the duty doctor's words again and again. Much calmer already, she was glad of her decision not to go to the hospital. Sometimes her mind became so clear, that it was as if she had full understanding of everything that came by her; all seemed understandable to her, if not acceptable.

When the time for Maud's psychological assessment actually came, she had subconsciously treated it with such importance that she felt it was a tidemark of her illness. There was great disappointment, therefore, when she found out the truth of the meeting; a psychotherapy meeting, another endless seam of questions identical to those already asked by about five different doctors.

All through the appointment, she tried to concentrate herself on the present in order to remove the dissatisfaction created. When the time was up, she refused to have another appointment made. There was no way that she would risk building up her hopes again when all it boiled down to was an interview that led nowhere. She hated the idea of milestones in her everyday life, could not be free when appointments loomed ahead.

The psychotherapist was small and wiry with frizzy hair and spectacles too large for her thin-lipped face. Maud was relieved not to have to see her again. She felt that the time they had spent together was merely a verbal battle, wordplay and who could score points off the other. Maud had used analogy to show how talking things over could not change matters: 'I understand fully why I have periods every month, but there's nothing I can do to change it.'

'You can stop eating,' came the answer, with only parallel understanding.

She wore a blue Lycra dress and blue opaque tights so that her legs were blue. They reminded Maud of varicose veins. She was slightly disgusted by the legs and kept staring at them discreetly throughout the hour's talk.

Maud had postponed her meeting with Grumer until that with the psychotherapist was over. She wanted to feel that she was dealing with things one at a time.

She booked the seats for *Last Tango in Paris*, and then called him at work to tell him when to meet her. As it was, they met outside the cinema, half an hour before the programme commenced.

She did not wear the jeans that had lately become her sole uniform, but a pair of black cigarette pants and a colourful Pucci top. Grumer wore the same suit and tie that she only knew him in and was waiting when she arrived.

'Hello,' she greeted, a little uneasy at his presence, 'how are things?'

'Fine.' He nodded. 'I haven't ever seen this film, know what it's about though.'

'I suppose you're wondering about its relevance to us being here now.'

He nodded, holding open the heavy glass door for her and guiding her through with his hand on the small of her back. She shuddered at this and hurried into the building, determined that she would have to keep a distance from him so that he would not touch her.

She turned to him. 'Its only relevance is that I went to see the film with two friends, only one of which I knew before arriving here. It was a bit like the meeting that we have just had, only there were two of us today. It was also like the meeting in the film, only there were three of us then.' She smiled, looking for a reaction.

'All I know of *Last Tango* is that it's about two people who meet and do not know each other's name. They go always to the same building, where they develop a sexual relationship. They have perfectly normal lives aside from this.'

'Well, we'll watch the film in a few minutes, but that's about the basis for the story.'

'So where do you and your two friends come into it?'

Collecting their tickets from the small booking office, they climbed the red-plush stairs and found their way in the wall-to-wall red plush to their screen, No. 2.

Maud guided Grumer to the back row. 'I want to talk,' she explained, and she felt the hotness of his breath close to her neck so that the wispy hairs there tickled her.

'We aren't really going to watch the film, only I thought it would bring back memories if I were to relive the occasion.' The curtains swished to a close and then reopened, and the film credits began to roll.

'My good friend Yasmin asked me to help her. She and a

78

man were in love, only they found the attraction they had for each other was ruining the relationship. Sex was all they could think about; they needed somebody to act as a mediator between them, to try and cool their emotions. I agreed to take on this responsibility.'

Grumer was startled at this revelation. 'What do you mean by mediator?' he asked. 'How did you fulfil this task?'

'I had not met Alan before the evening when we went, all three, to see *Last Tango in Paris*. They had seen it a few weeks before on their own. Only they wanted to recreate the experience with me in the same way as we are recreating that particular experience today. Alan and I did not greet each other. It was enough that we knew each other through Yasmin. We began to watch the film, myself sitting between the two of them. Then Yasmin held my hand and made a sign for me to do the same with Alan. It was a lovely feeling, the three of us creating an energy field in this way. You know, I could actually feel what was between them being conducted through myself.' Maud chuckled, then reached for Grumer's hand.

'We sat like that for a few minutes, and then Yasmin began to stroke my thigh. Very gently, as if her fingers were made of feathers. The effect through the cotton of these trousers, I was dressed exactly as I am today, was scintillating. And she did not need to tell me to pass the effect on to Alan. I looked at him and he was staring ahead at the screen. I'm not sure whether he was aware that it was me and not Yasmin who was touching him, or if he cared about it. Then, with the hand that clasped mine, Yasmin began to dig her long nails into my flesh and I too tried to dig my shorter nails into his.

'They didn't ask me directly to join them in their relationship, but Yasmin's behaviour during the film was adequate in its suggestion of what should happen between the three of us. And it all seemed so natural to us.' Maud stopped, hooking a strand of hair with her third finger and tucking it behind her ear.

'Then she brought my hand up to her mouth and sank her teeth slowly into my knuckles.' Maud took Grumer's hand and illustrated this.

'What effect did it have on you?' he asked, bringing their hands down to his side.

'Oh, I didn't think about it at the time, but the passion on the screen was more realistic than it could have otherwise been.'

She unclasped her hand from Grumer's and moved it along to his thigh, where she let it rest. He shifted uncomfortably in his seat and out of the corner of her eye, she saw that he ran his fingers round the inside of his collar.

'I turned to Yasmin, and we kissed.'

Grumer looked at her enquiringly.

'Full on the lips,' Maud added, 'it was the first time that I had ever kissed a woman. I wasn't expecting it to be any different from a man's kiss, you see it wasn't something I had thought about.'

'And . . .' Grumer hurried her speech on.

'Well, it was quite a shock actually. Her lips tasted of balm; apricot. And her lips were soft and full. I have to say that I was repulsed at first. I would have preferred kissing Alan, except that he was not as ready as the two of us to enter into a relationship.' Maud laughed. 'It was a really crazy experience,' she cried. 'There I was, sandwiched between the two of them, unsure of quite what to do, taking my orders from Yasmin, and passing them on to Alan. I was their vehicle.' She looked at Grumer, and saw his profile. He seemed to be watching the screen intently.

'Of course, it's something that can't really be explained. And there are only the two of us here. You need to experience it to understand how it happened, what it meant.'

'Well, my dear, I don't want to put the dampers on everything, but it's quite a common thing to happen. Threesomes. A little more personal than a full-blown orgy, of course, and a lot less common than wife swapping. That's all I can say.'

Maud sensed that he was trying to wind her up. She felt that perhaps he did not believe she was disclosing all of her knowledge. She also thought that it was a possibility that he was jealous. After all, she had made no indication of wanting him.

'Have you ever tried it?' she asked suddenly, turning towards him.

He looked down at his hands, picking at the ragged cuticle of his thumb.

'It's not something that I've ever even thought about. Certainly, I can't imagine my wife wanting to take part.'

'But yourself?' Maud persisted.

'Maybe.' He refused to commit himself to an answer.

Maud sighed and turned again to face the screen.

'When I put on weight, I pretended that I was Maria Schneider. Well, actually the character in this film, more than just the actress. What do you think? She's got a fabulous figure.'

'Yes. Skinny and plump all at once,' Grumer responded.

'Yasmin told me that when she first came to see the film with Alan, he tried buggering her straight after. They never keep butter, though, Alan's trying to lower his cholesterol. So they used Flora instead. What a scream!!' She gave a high pitched laugh. Completely false, thought Grumer.

'Medically speaking, I would have thought margarine would be a lot easier. A far better lubricant than butter.'

'You're missing the point as usual,' Maud complained. 'Where's the sensuality in a plastic tub of marg? Anyway, she said it was awful. Neither of them came.'

'So. What happened next between you three?'

'I forced my hand down Alan's trousers. Yasmin whispered in my ear for me to do that. He had an erection. The butter scene had just passed. Poor Alan, the frustration of watching that scene and then becoming impotent in your starring moment . . . then a strange thing happened.' Her voice changed, she seemed quiet, free from her former ebullience. 'They both leaned towards me, and bit my cheek.'

'Metaphorical?' Grumer suggested. 'A mating symbol, perhaps.'

'When we left, shortly afterwards, none of us spoke. I wasn't sure we'd ever all meet up again until Yasmin called me about two weeks later. That was when I had the idea of using Hotel 167.'

'167, what's that?' he asked as they collected their coats piled on the next seat and moved out of the carpeted row towards the exit.

'Later,' Maud whispered, and they left the cinema, wordless.

Grumer held open the door of his Mazda for Maud and she slumped into the low seat. Then he made his way round to the driver's side and she leant across to unlock it. When he slid in, there was a pause before he switched on the ignition.

'I think I'll have to explain to you exactly who Yasmin is,' Maud proposed, and Grumer let the engine warm up for a few minutes as he listened to her story.

'She's actually the mother of a friend of mine. A friend whom I haven't seen for three years.' Maud pulled the sleeve of her sweater down over her fist and rolled a stray thread between finger and thumb.

'I was phoned up out of the blue during the summer of '90. It was Alex's mother, Yasmin. Her daughter had left home without warning, they didn't know how to get hold of her, but they needed my help. Yasmin had managed to find the number of her daughter's boyfriend in France, and, as I spoke the language fluently, asked me to call up to see if Alex was staying with him there. I did so and eventually we found out that that was what had happened. It was a great relief to Yasmin and Alex's father, Martin.'

Maud rubbed her side window with two fingers, wiping away the mist so that a small porthole was left. She looked out on to the street, at the people pouring out of the cinema, or waiting under the restaurant awnings next door to be collected.

'Yasmin doesn't see her daughter much nowadays. The house was small and it was oppressive for Alex, living with her parents. Especially since she was an only child. They were over protective of her, you see. And Martin's job isn't well paid; he's an accountant. Yasmin, though, she's a sometime actress. Gets jobs doing voice overs or bit parts in commercials.' Maud's voice changed and there was disguised pride in her voice. 'You've probably seen her, in the ad for sofa beds – long blonde hair, green eyes . . .'

Grumer didn't answer, so she continued. 'Well, I became very close to Yasmin, she was depressed quite a lot about the split between herself and her daughter. They had been so close the years building up to when she left.'

'What's this got to do with you and Alan, though,' Grumer asked, 'and who is Alan if she's got a husband called Martin?'

'Oh, she doesn't sleep with Martin,' Maud explained, 'they have a business arrangement. They married because they wanted a child and they trusted each other not to leave if anything went wrong. As it is, that aspect of their relationship worked well. Yasmin kept her affairs secret from her daughter, and I don't think Martin actually had any. I can imagine that accountancy can be a very invasive job. Too tiring to allow for any personal life. Anyway the mentality that veers towards accountancy is self-explanatory in that department.' She laughed, lightening the atmosphere between herself and the psychiatrist.

'You know, I don't actually think of you as my psychiatrist any more,' she revealed, 'funny, isn't it? Our relationship was so formal before we got to know each other like this.'

'So tell me about Alan,' he interrupted, switching off the engine and leaning back in his seat. He adjusted the head rest so that it cradled the top of his neck.

'Alan is one of Yasmin's lovers. Her most important lover.'

'She has several at once?'

'At the moment, yes, though I think all that would change if he agreed to go on seeing her on a regular basis.'

'So what's the big problem between them?'

Maud sighed. 'I don't really know; you see, although I know Yasmin intimately, I know very little of Alan. He was in the army, that much I'm sure of, and he retired ten years ago. Since then he's been involved in freelance publishing. Made quite a profit with virtually no employees. Only hire-and-fire temps under him. I think that's the secret to his recent expansion. Anyway, he's crazy about Yasmin, but refuses to see her. She can't understand why, but I think I know. He needs to be in control, feel that he's completely independent, which he can't do when Yasmin's there. She has such an effect on him. Women are different from men. They like to be permanently in love, or at least the majority do. For men, they either have affairs on a casual basis, or feel that they want to settle down.

And he's already been married once, he's got two grown-up children. I guess he feels too old to take the plunge again.'

'But he wouldn't have to marry her.'

'I know that, but it's still a threat to feel the way he does about Yasmin. Anyway, that's the story. Yasmin felt that by bringing me into the picture, they might be able to look at each other more objectively.

'Normally they can't keep their hands off each other. They have to if I'm there. They seem to restrict their passion, and deal with each other through me. Nothing is wasted.'

'It's a strange thing for them to expect of you, though.' Grumer frowned, not understanding quite why this three-way relationship had been formed.

'I don't think so.' She smiled as she considered the past. 'You see it's a long time since I've had a relationship with anyone. I don't seem to find men attractive enough. But with three, it's not so much to do with the physical attraction, so much as the taboo of the situation. That in itself is a real turn on. And then we all have a lot of fondness for each other. A special love that wouldn't exist if only any two of us were present. There's more a sense of sharing the physical as opposed to selfish lust.'

'It seems odd to me,' was Grumer's response, 'and I'm used to some pretty strange set ups. Usually kinks, though, I guess, or rather sexual anomalies, as they are referred to professionally.'

'So would you say that this is one of those? A sexual anomaly, I mean.'

'It depends.' He stroked the roots of his beard. 'If you are being treated by the other two as a sort of surrogate daughter, then, yes, I'd say that was a little unwholesome.'

'Oh no, I'd say I was more a surrogate lover than a daughter to them,' she interjected, the intensity in her eyes suggesting that she wanted Grumer's blessing as to the purity of the association. It was clearly something that she valued very deeply, and Grumer was immediately aware of this.

'It's not entirely ethical, but then who's to say what's right and what's wrong. In my opinion, love of any kind, so long as none of the parties gets hurt, is something to be praised.'

'Good, I'm glad you see it like that,' Maud responded, reassured, 'that's how we look at it. Though the relationship was an active one, not at all analytical.'

Maud looked across at Grumer now, wondering whether there was any jealousy at such relations as he was to be denied. She wondered if he even knew as much, or if he expected favours at all. She decided that he probably did; she could not imagine that he was interested in her purely as a means to study a case history in a more profound way. Besides, he would not be able to make others aware of this knowledge, he'd be struck off for sure. He was committing a mortal sin as far as psychiatry went and of course he was aware of that much.

'You've never had anything like that happen to you?' she asked, interested in his personal life.

He shook his head. 'I haven't even had many lovers in my lifetime. Not since I was married anyway.'

'But now?' She was testing him, and he knew as much.

'Not now, not ever,' was all that he said.

There was a full bottle of Evian rolling under the seat.

'For the car?' she asked, dragging it up by the see-through plastic lid.

'Yes. It's only tap water.'

Maud unscrewed the bottle and held it up to her lips, tilting her head right back and sucking the cool water down her throat in great gulps.

86

Replacing the bottle, she wiped her lips with the back of her hand, feeling the slight slimy covering of saliva that coated her formerly dry mouth.

'Want some?' she asked, and he shook his head.

Resuming the monologue about Alan and Yasmin, she continued. 'Anyway, it wasn't a direct decision that Yasmin made with me. We used to talk for ages about her and Alan. It was really interesting. I felt myself attracted to him without even having met him. Of course, that's purely narcissistic, he was in my mind an extension of myself.'

From the indication that Grumer made, he was clearly impressed with her reasoning.

'I was so angry that he was throwing away the love that they shared. It was such a self-centred thing to do. You see, it was something that belonged to them both and neither should have been able to ruin it. Especially out of cowardice.' Maud turned her watch face round to the inside of her wrist. Tracing its circumference, she added, 'I felt at that time that I needed to speak to Alan on her behalf. Let him know what a mistake he was making. It had happened to him in a previous relationship, he actually told Yasmin that. He had been going out with a woman while he was married, on and off for seven years. She had wanted to move in with him, but of course he was not ready to make the commitment. Not ready when they met, and not ready seven years later. When she finally woke up to herself, she refused to have anything more to do with him. She had had enough pain and was beginning to make a new life for herself. She just didn't want to jeopardize that when he had let her down so many times. That's what really hit me. The fact that he could repeat the mistake. Perhaps it was deliberate, a sort of masochism. Only it wasn't acceptable, because he was hurting my friend at the same time as he hurt himself.' Maud shuddered.

'Are you cold?' Grumer suggested.

She shook her head and continued: 'Anyway, first we began to talk of my meeting him as a sort of joke. We had discussed him so much, it was as if we were beginning to share him. And we wanted him to be part of this sensation too.'

'So that's what you did.'

'Not at first. We thought initially that maybe I could spy on him at their next meeting. But then if he found out, or if I wanted to meet him at a later date, it just wouldn't work. So Yasmin suggested the idea of a threesome to him. She made it sound as if she and he would be helping me out. Because it was so long since I had known anyone sexually. It's true, I don't have that many friends. She told him that it would build up my confidence to meet a man who I knew wasn't a threat. Because, of course, she was going out with him.'

'I don't understand, though. I thought you said your first meeting was to see *Last Tango in Paris*?'

'Well, it follows, doesn't it? I mean it was just a really subtle way of introducing us to each other. And without having to explain to him what was to be had out of the relationship.

'It's such an erotic film. We knew that none of us could resist. Especially in the back row.' She gave an uncontrollable wide grin. 'It was a joke really. Neither Yasmin nor I were aware of the full effects that the film would have on us. It all progressed naturally.'

'And you left each other directly that the film was over?' he asked.

'Well, I left them together. Yasmin refused to let Alan discuss me or what was happening between us all. From that point, we were all to live existentially. That is to say, none of us talked about the three of us. We just let it happen.'

'What happened next?' Grumer wanted to know. 'Who made the next move: I suppose it was you and Yasmin?'

'We'll leave that to our next meeting. When are you free?'

'Any time you say,' he rolled down his window and spat out on to the street, as, Maud thought, a display of his masculinity.

'Next week then. We'll meet at Sloane Square tube station, but I'll call you nearer the time. I'll get a bus home.' And she opened the car door, bending across the seat to give him a kiss on the cheek. He grabbed her hand and she drew it away roughly.

Once out on the pavement she let the door slam to and made her way to the nearest bus stop.

She knew that Grumer was already getting eager, that he wanted to know everything about the relationship with Yasmin and Alan. He was turned on too, by it, she could tell. Smiling to herself, she hailed the next bus and hauled herself on.

Maud had supposed that her dealings with Grumer would help her psychologically.

She thought that control over the psychiatrist would gain her a greater feeling of power over herself: that somehow it would prove to her that doctors were as weak as any human beings and that she didn't need to have anything to do with them.

Things didn't quite work out that way, though, and it was only a few days later when once again Maud was struck with such a negative urge that she felt like putting an end to her life there and then.

She had only just woken up when the sensation came about. She was watching TV in the kitchen. The frustration built up gradually, so that at first she was unable to concentrate her mind on anything other than what she was going through at present. And then not even as much as that, for she became ruled by her physicality.

Pacing up and down the kitchen she pulled the lid off the bread tin and yanked out the plastic bagged loaf of sliced bread. Breaking off an edge of crust, she stuffed this in her mouth, but was unable to chew. Opening the window, she threw the crust out to the birds and then proceeded to tear up the rest of that slice. An enormous woodpigeon landed on the sill, almost as large as Maud's head. He was so fat that he could hardly fit on the ledge and had to keep flapping his wings to keep balance. No other birds flew down into the garden while the woodpigeons were there, so Maud did her best to frighten him away.

Sitting down, she tried the deep-breathing exercises that a friend had shown her. It was impossible, she couldn't even get her breath. Everything seemed impossible that day. And the day seemed impossibly long. Minutes and hours of minutes and a whole day of hours of minutes: and of seconds. She began to panic and paced with gathered speed the length of the room. Pausing at the fridge, she took down her bottle of Flupenthixol. Since she had stopped taking them, there were over eighty left in the bottle. Though she shouldn't actually take as many as that or she would simply vomit them out. The idea of choking on her own vomit seemed an utterly pointless way to die. Hardly dramatic, more a minor accident.

Sitting down at the table, Maud scraped her chair in until she was tightly lodged; comfortable. Then she tipped out the faintly bile-coloured tablets on to the oilskin tablecloth. Separating them into groups of ten she counted. Eighty-six pills. She discarded three groups of ten and six individual tablets; that left fifty. Fifty seemed like a good number. She collected the tablets once more in the bottle and threw the discarded ones down the waste-disposal unit. Holding the bottle to her lips, she thought to herself: 'Now if I can just swallow these, I'll be able to lie down and wait for them to take effect. It will be so easy, they'll make me drowsy at once. How shall I do it? A glass of water, I think.' And she went to fetch a glass of water, filling it at the sink.

A suicide note? she joked to herself. No, that's a little too pretentious, and she slunk into her seat, the glass of water and the tinted plastic bottle of pills set in front of her.

How many gulps am I going to have to take? she wondered. She wanted to be sure of the exact process before it happened. Three, probably. One gulp of pills then one of water. A second of each and then the final one. All washed down nicely, thank you very much and time for bed.

I don't have the nerve, she thought to herself a few seconds later. I can't believe this, I want to, need to get it over with and I'm too chicken. Perhaps that means that I don't want to die. But there's no other way out, she shrieked inside, as she replaced the screw-on cap and swallowed the water on its own. Shit fuck, she thought, what a shit fuck thing to happen to me. Shit fuck shit fuck shit fuck, she repeated at great speed to herself. Now what? Now all finished, nothing left to be done. She went downstairs to her bedroom. Climbing under the duvet, she tried to relax. She pretended that she had actually taken the pills, that she was lain down, ready to die. What if she had taken the pills and just couldn't remember? It could be a trick of her imagination. And then she would be found dead and thought to have committed suicide when it was all an accident. A big, bloody, empty accident. No I haven't taken them, she reassured, only in my mind they're already working.

And eyes closed, she left her mouth open, to breathe as if in great difficulty. You see, she was dying, she really was. Because she couldn't live any longer, it was killing her. Dashing off the covers, she rose from the bed. I can't stand this any longer, no more, no fucking more, and again she began to pace. Up and down, up and down, nothing to catch her interest, to bring her once more to pacified reality. Life was for her, at that moment, a series of pacing, up and down, and faster and faster, and not even the rhythm or the repetition could help.

Racing up the stairs two at a time, holding on to the banister, she arrived at the drawing-room door. Pushing it open she went straight to the phone. I'm going to have to telephone, was her decision. Holding her breath, she dialled the numbers, ten digits because it was an 081 code.

'Hello, King George's,' came the voice at the other end.

'Can I speak to the duty doctor, please?' she asked, forcing the words out.

'Hold on, please. I'll just try and locate him.' The voice at the other end was dry and uninterested. Maud didn't care that it was a Sunday. It was after all his job.

'Hold on, please,' came the same voice, and Maud waited.

Several minutes passed and she began to wonder whether she had been inadvertently cut off. But she was too scared to put the receiver down in case she didn't dare call again. So she waited.

Finally, a new voice came on the line. 'Hello, I'm the senior registrar.' The voice was coolly pleasant. Maud tilted her head, she warmed to it.

'Hi, I'm a patient of Dr Nixon.' It was the speech that she had planned out the last time that she had called. 'He told me to call this number if ever I felt unwell.'

'Right, and your name is?'

'Maud Faulkes.'

'Ah, yes, so what exactly is the matter? I understand that you called about a week ago.'

'Yes.'

'And how are you feeling at the moment?' The voice sounded concerned.

Maud felt silly. 'I'm feeling really depressed,' she answered, 'depressed and frustrated.'

'I see. Would you like to come down and see me?'

'OK.' Maud was suddenly submissive.

'You could come down now if you like,' he told her.

'Oh, I'll be all right until tomorrow morning.' She felt eased by the kindness of the voice, its willingness to help.

'If you're sure.'

'Yes, I'm quite sure,' she decided.

'Right, well if you could come down at eleven o'clock tomorrow, I'll be there to see you. My name's Dr Richards.'

'Thanks a lot.' Maud was gratified and relieved. The appointment gave her something to cling to.

'Goodbye.' She ended the conversation and replaced the receiver, suddenly able to breathe again, filled with a curiosity to know what Dr Richards was like.

The next day, as she made her way to King George's, Maud felt none of the apprehension that she usually experienced prior to an appointment. Although she was now taking a new capsule, a tranquillizer called Stelazine, she felt that this had nothing to do with the strange calmness that she felt. When her GP had agreed with her psychiatrist that she should try this medication, she had been wholeheartedly against it. A few days previously however, her mood had been such that she had called up her doctor, and asked him to leave the prescription with the receptionists for her to collect. Having stopped in a library to look up Stelazine in a medical publication, she had found that she had been prescribed a high dose, recommended for schizophrenics. Fortunately, she had faith enough in herself to know that she did not suffer from that particular illness.

When she arrived at King George's, Maud weaved her way through the cloister of old buildings and towards the Mental Health Unit. Once there, she stuck her head through the wooden frame of the reception.

'I've an appointment at eleven,' she stated to the man behind the desk. He always looked the same, even his clothes did not distinguish him from one day to the next.

'Who with?' he asked.

'Dr Richards?' Maud was now unsure of his name.

'And your name is?'

'Maud Faulkes,' she replied, studying the black tuft close to his forehead that had defied his receding hairline.

'Take a seat, please,' and accordingly she made her way round the back of the reception to the waiting room.

She always sat at the same table, because it was the only table that did not have low chairs round it. She would of course have preferred one of the comfortable armchairs, but was too aware of the difficulties that could be experienced when it came to getting up. She did not want to embarrass herself in front of any members of the staff.

The wait was long; there was a large round clock on the wall and Maud kept turning her head to check on the time. She had specially worn a wristwatch so that she wouldn't be late, but, in her anxiety, forgot about this. And so, every few minutes, she turned her head round sharply to gaze at the minimally moving minute hand.

It was almost an hour later when a man dressed in a badly cut suit sauntered up to her.

'Maud Faulkes?' he asked.

She nodded and he continued, 'I'm Dr Richards,' extending his hand as he leant towards her. She shook it and then raised herself from the chair, glad that she had chosen the upright one.

Maud followed Dr Richards to the small room where her previous appointments had been conducted.

He seemed a fairly tall man from his build, although strangely he was half an inch shorter than Maud. She herself was five foot eight and she decided it was his good looks and confidence that lent him height.

When he opened the door, Maud saw that the social worker was already seated inside. She reminded Maud of a patch of damp on a wall that was unexpected until seen and remembered. A mouldy patch at that, she thought as she greeted the ubiquitous Jenny, whose smile was a dusting of caster sugar.

'You've met Jenny.' Dr Richards began his introduction, to be cut short by the two of them as they met once more with a grin.

'Yes, we know each other,' Maud assured him, noting how pleased Jenny seemed that she was able to say as much.

'How are you feeling today, then?' Dr Richards asked when they sat down. Maud noticed that although she and the doctor had crossed their legs in opposite directions, their knees almost met. Jenny sat with both feet firmly on the ground, her above the knee skirt riding up so that Maud could see the fleshiness of her inner thigh. She noticed that Jenny had not shaved her lower legs and was repulsed at the hair caught beneath the meshy tights.

'Actually I'm feeling a great deal better today,' she informed him. Indeed she had considered cancelling the appointment earlier that morning, quite guilty that she should be in such good spirits after yesterday's phone call.

'What about yesterday, tell me how you felt then,' and Maud studied the doctor's eyes, how the curled lashes that circled them made him appear slightly girlish despite the roughness of his skin and the pallor of his lips.

'Yesterday was terrible,' she admitted. 'I'm not sure whether today I don't feel better because of the Stelazine that I've started to take.'

'How long have you taken that for?' Jenny interjected.

Maud turned to her. 'Only a couple of days, I'm not even sure that it can work that quickly.'

'But before you started taking it?' Richards resumed his questioning.

'I felt really depressed. Also frustrated. I couldn't do a thing. I can't believe how I felt now, it doesn't seem that yesterday was part of me at all. I actually thought that the only way to put a stop to how I felt was to put an end to myself.'

Richards sighed, cocking his head to one side. 'And have you thought about how you would have done that?' he asked.

'Well, I'm sure everyone plans out how they would die if they wanted to at some point in their lives. Everybody needs to be prepared,' Maud reasoned.

'Yes, that's true to an extent, but they don't dwell on death, that's not normal.'

'Well, I thought about pills, only I know that's hard because either you take too many and vomit them out or not enough and risk ending up a vegetable.' She grinned and Richards joined her.

'I thought you were supposed to destroy those pills,' Jenny reprimanded.

'There didn't seem to be any point; you see my father takes all sorts of pills for his heart – Quinidine, Digoxin, Verapamil' – she looked at the doctor, who seemed fairly impressed at this knowledge – 'and I could always take those if I wanted to. Anyway, I'd rather die of anti–depressants than from an induced heart attack, if you know what I mean.'

Maud felt that she was becoming too chirpy and tried to calm herself down. But it was as if the capsule of Stelazine had prevented a hysterical mood and lessened it so that now instead she was hyperactive.

'Have you thought of any other ways?' he asked. Maud thought of the cuts she had made on her arm the night before. She wanted to show them off to him, so that he would feel protective of her; on the other hand, she didn't want to appear that she had done them deliberately as a form of exhibitionism.

'Well, there's cutting, but I don't think I could negotiate my veins.' She shuddered as she thought of a film in which a boy had snipped through his veins with a razor blade; unforgettable because the sound that it had made was that of scissors cutting a thick flower stem.

'And then there's hanging, but I don't have a beam in the house.' She paused. 'I think I'd have to go for the pills. Easier than throwing yourself off a tall building, and less selfish than going in front of a tube train.'

Dr Richards laughed and Jenny remained reactionless. Maud was pleased because she seemed to have succeeded in weaning him across to her way of thinking. He was almost proud of her at this point, it seemed to her.

'How long were you on anti–depressants for?' came his next question.

'I've tried three or four kinds,' she explained, 'but only for a maximum course of six weeks.'

'That doesn't seem long enough for a course to start working.' Pulling the left flap of his jacket across his body, he continued, 'Which ones have you tried, can you remember?'

Maud nodded, and rattled off the list. 'Prothiaden for a couple of weeks. Clomipramine for about the same time, maybe a little longer, and then the Amitrip lasted for six or seven weeks.'

The doctor nodded, his pen poised at the manila sheet for note taking. As she glanced down at it she saw that unlike at her previous meetings he had not made any notes.

'Right, well, I think we ought to get you on a course of a more modern anti-depressant. What sort of side effects were you experiencing on the Amitriptyline?' he asked, putting down his pen and slotting the fingers of both hands together.

'All of them really,' she laughed, nervously. 'I was gaining weight, suffered from blurred vision, shaking, hot flushes . . .'

'Dry mouth, constipation?' he suggested and she nodded, silent.

'So, the whole run of them really. That makes it very difficult to complete the course.' He paused, thinking to himself. 'But really, with the newer medication, there's no need to experience any of those side effects, especially the disturbing ones like the weight gain and the blurred vision. I know you said you didn't want to start taking pills again, but it might help if you let the course last long enough.'

He looked at her, questioning, and she responded accordingly: 'I guess it's worth trying another type of pill. If you really think that it might help.' Maud noticed the deep laughter lines round his mouth and saw them crinkle up into a professional smile.

'If you come in tomorrow morning, say at the same time

as this morning, then I'll ask someone to show you round the day centre. And I'll discuss the new medication with you, OK?' and there was the smile again.

'Jenny, have you got any further questions that you'd like to put to Maud?' and in response she shook her head, the bobbed blonde hair dancing so that it didn't quite catch up, but halted with a swing.

'Actually, yes, I wonder,' she turned to Maud, 'you do seem a lot livelier since you stopped taking the Amitriptyline. Do you feel that you've noticed that?'

Maud considered for a few moments. 'I can't tell if it's because of the Amitriptyline or maybe something to do with the new capsule that I've been taking.'

'The Stelazine spansule,' mused Jenny. 'Well whatever it is, she does seem much better than when we last met,' she assured the doctor, pleased at her own observation; as if Maud only existed for the benefit of Jenny's being able to enjoy her job, thrive in looking after others.

'Right,' Dr Richards concluded and Maud knew that this was her cue to leave.

'Thanks a lot,' she addressed Richards, shaking the hand that he held out to her. She wished that he hadn't, for his dry confident palm absorbed the muggy sweat of hers. He didn't seem to notice on the surface but she was sure that's what he was thinking.

'Goodbye,' she said in Jenny's direction, walking across to the door, her hand soon on the knob. She had a phobia about opening doors. If ever she was in an unknown car, she checked for the handle throughout the journey so that she should not embarrass herself when it came to getting out. She clenched her teeth that the door of the little conference room would not stick. It didn't and once again she found herself breathing in the air of the hospital gardens. The outside of the hospital was something that she greatly appreciated, because it was all that she thought of during one of her hairy meetings. She hated feeling boxed in and cornered as she answered question after question; especially when it meant that she was sandwiched between one of the doctors and the social worker. Then she felt really trapped.

All that day she was looking forward to seeing Richards again. There were less than twenty-four hours to wait. She washed herself carefully and made sure that she had clean clothes to wear, at the same time knowing that she was making a big deal out of something insignificant. Or at least, significant only to her.

When the day turned into the next and she found herself once more at King George's, the wait to see Richards built up anxiously in her mind. Sitting on her upright chair at the third table, she began to wonder whether she was always kept waiting so that she could be monitored in this room by a hidden camera. Suddenly a wave of embarrassment overcame her as she thought of the way she had been checking herself preparatorily, daubing salve on to her lips, tucking the hair behind her ears and rearranging the shoulder-bag that lay on her lap, huddled like a puppy.

The receptionist poked his head round the door. 'Dr Richards says he's going to be a little late and do you mind waiting another fifteen to twenty minutes for him?'

Maud's heart leapt a little, the sensation that of free-falling when on the edge of sleep.

'No, that's fine,' came her assurance, before turning back to the white plastic wall clock that kept vigil with her.

Trying not to watch the slow motion of the second hand, Maud turned her attention to the pile of newsletters on the table in front of her. Picking them up, one after the other, and flicking through, she had read excerpts of three before realizing that they were all copies of each other. Presumably they had been piled there so that people could take them away to read, or perhaps as a means of furnishing the bare room. There was nobody in the coffee bar that day. It opened from one to four most days and Maud read the notice that hung on its door. 'The coffee bar is only for the use of those patients who are awaiting an appointment with a member of staff.'

She wondered where the in-patients spent their days if such limits were placed on hospital property.

It was with relief that she realized how close she had come to being admitted. It was only now that she understood the importance of keeping her emotions to herself and not allowing the hospital to become too involved. That was a sure fire way to be admitted. Thank Heaven she had not asked to become an in-patient, something that her doctor had suggested that she do. She did not trust that once that happened, the staff wouldn't try to keep her in indefinitely.

As she waited, there was a build up of agitation within her. She began to stretch her arms forward at regular intervals. Clenching the muscles of her buttocks, she could feel her bowels weakening to a movement. She concentrated, studying the degree to which her stomach lurched upwards, digging her diaphragm, as the minutes passed. Minutes and more minutes, until at last the very male shadow of Dr Richards came towards her. She was sure that he had a complex about his height and was pleased that seeing her above him must make him nervous of her. When she looked into his face she saw that he was not as good looking as she had suspected him of being the day before. Perhaps it just seemed that way because all of the other psychiatrists that she had known had been of strange appearances. This man looked wholesome. He looked as if he enjoyed women. Not like the doctor with the eyes screwed into his head. Unlike he who had reminded her of a leprechaun. Certainly, he bore no resemblance to the Germanic Grumer, whose great habit was to tickle his beard as he spoke. Perhaps he liked to tickle his wife's chest with it when they were in bed together. Maud chuckled inwardly, her mood heightening, her fingers drumming motionless and her body bent still. 'Hello, Maud,' he greeted, coming to a stop in front of her. Immediately she was shy in front of him, as if they had never fallen into such easy conversation the previous day. 'Hi,' she returned, controlling the mouth that began to turn into a smile. She would not let Richards see how much she admired him. You see she was only beginning to trust him, although she felt that this was the man her GP had been talking about when he suggested that she start a relationship with a psychiatrist. Maud felt sure that it was he who was indirectly spoken of.

'How are you feeling today?' he asked as she gathered up her cloth bag and swung it over her shoulder, sack-like. There was nothing in the bag and only very little in the way of belongings in the zipped front pocket. Consequently, it skulked behind her as if ashamed of itself.

'I'm OK today,' she told him, 'but the Stelazine is definitely making me hyperactive.'

'Hyperactive?' The doctor was clearly surprised, for the Stelazine was a heavy tranquillizer. Maud explained to him her theory about the capsule calming her hysterics so that she was reduced to a state of jitters. He seemed to understand her way of looking at things, though he thought that this was no explanation.

'I think we'll go round to the day centre first. I'm sorry I had to keep you waiting so long,' he apologized, and once again Maud wondered whether this was all part of the ruse. The plan to spy on her in the waiting room. An invasion of privacy. 'That's all right, it wasn't too long,' she responded, getting up from her seat and following him out of the waiting room. She was pleased that that day no one had come in to talk to her. She felt sure that she would have blushed deeply, the way she almost had the last time that it happened.

The day centre was in a modern block round the back of the main building. It looked like a temporary construction, similar to those made on wheels out of what appeared to be thick-painted card.

Opening the door and guiding her through, there was a row of bright orange plastic chairs opposite where he told her to wait while he spoke to the man in charge. She took her seat at the far end of the row, one of the two remaining that were vacant.

Promptly a man came towards her and sat down. Maud was busy fixing one of her shoulder straps. It had come undone and hung loose to her embarrassment as she had walked with Dr Richards across the courtyard.

'Are you a nurse or a patient?' the young man asked. He wore a blue shell-suit that crinkled round his knees like an accordion as he sat.

'An out-patient,' she responded, not looking up. Unwilling to converse.

'Me too,' came his reply and there he remained for several

minutes until he realized that there was no more to be squeezed from her.

He got up and left and another man took his place. Foreign looking, he had dark olive skin and a thick black moustache, virile looking. Maud thought how strange it was that moustaches usually made men look submissive as if they had grown them to hide behind, like a hedgerow round a communal garden. This man's rendered him more virile. He looked ahead as he fumbled with the wrapping of a canvas. Unsure, Maud stared secretly at him without moving her eyes from the wall opposite on which they were fixed. He reminded her of her old art teacher at school. The *lycée* was near by, in South Kensington, so it could have been him. A mixture of French and Arabic. As Dr Richards came out of the head office, this man greeted him congenially.

'Dr Richards, how are you?'

'Hello, Achmed,' the greeting was returned, 'nice to see you today,' and he crossed over to where Maud was sitting.

'Jeremy's going to show you round the day centre and maybe make another appointment to see you tomorrow,' he confided. 'When you've finished make another appointment to see Dr Nixon,' and with that he vanished, deserting Maud, leaving her to a stranger, she whom he knew had trouble adapting to changes. Why had he treated her thus?

Jeremy approached, very young and skinny in black denim drainpipes, a red long-sleeved T-shirt and pointy black shoes. His lank hair curled round his neck and hung in stripes as if it had been highlighted and needed a wash.

He took Maud's hand limply and she was unable to shake it properly for fear that it should come off in her own. She was far stronger than he despite his height.

'Hallo, I'm Jeremy, and I'll be taking you round our day centre.' He grinned, like a goblin, the stature of an elf in his pointy clothes with his pointy features. He was the type of person who should have been heralded by the tinny ringing of bells. Tinnitus, yes he could have been a person who suited this condition.

First he led her to a room not unlike that in which Dr Richards had conducted his interview with Maud the day before. 'Sit down.' He waved his hand to one of the low armchairs that Maud detested and which seemed to plague this particular hospital. She couldn't understand how hospital furniture could be so deficient, especially considering the concentration of elderly or less able patients. She sat.

'Right, Dr Richards tells me that you are going to join our day centre.' He looked at her, matter of factly. Maud felt embarrassed as she spoke. 'Well, actually, he suggested that I come and have a look round. I'm not really sure that I do want to attend. I agreed that I'd visit it, though.'

'I see. So really I've got to sell it to you!' He laughed, producing a sheet of paper, printed with a timetable. Edging his seat towards her, they shared the diagram. 'Well, as you can see we have a great variety of workshops and classes that can be attended.' He indicated the boxes filled with writing and room numbers.

'Of course, you don't have to attend all of them, we can tailor the classes to fit your own needs,' he explained. Maud nodded, already repulsed by the idea. The timetable seemed worse than any that she had had during her educational life.

Maud followed his finger as they journeyed together along the list.

'Community meetings,' he began. 'Now these are held

every morning, as you can see.' He spoke lightheartedly, seeming to enjoy her company.

'They're held from nine o'clock until ten and everyone meets up to discuss the general running of the day's programme. It's a time when in-patients and out-patients mingle, try to get to know each other a little better. It also enables the staff to liaise more with the patients.'

'Right.' Again Maud nodded, unsure of her reaction, not wanting to appear too enthusiastic for fear that she should be cornered into joining any of the meetings.

'Don't look so worried,' he laughed, looking at her facial expression. 'You don't have to say anything if you don't want to. In any of these classes you have the opportunity to either participate or simply to sit back and listen.'

She nodded, 'Uh, huh,' leaning closer to the sheet, slightly more confident than before. She would not let Jeremy edge her into doing anything that she didn't want to do. He would not begin to control her like Dr Richards, who earlier had promised that they would discuss her prescription of a new anti-depressant together, and who had then proceeded to leave her with this skunk, promising only another appointment with Dr Nixon. She didn't understand why in the beginning he had led her to believe that they would be seeing more of one another. Did he suspect that her feelings for him weren't part of that ethical doctor-patient relationship? Was the hospital and in particular Dr Nixon and his 'team' simply trying to gauge the depth of her insecurity? She had had enough. No longer would they gain manipulation of her.

Jeremy picked up. 'Then on Mondays, as you can see, there's the women's group, which is self-explanatory. I can't tell you much about that because I've not yet managed to get in on the class,' he joked. Maud grinned wordlessly.

'You might be interested in the concentration group.' He turned to her. 'Dr Richards tells me that you often have trouble keeping your mind on any one thing. That sometimes you find yourself unable to do anything?'

Fuck Dr Richards, then aloud, 'Yes, I guess so. It might be a help for me to go to that,' she offered.

'Good,' he stated. 'Now art education is very popular. Everyone gets together and does painting and sketches. I think you saw some hanging on the walls as you came in.'

'There were some lovely pieces of painted pottery,' Maud remarked.

'Well, that might be something that you could think about joining.' She noticed how his fingers seemed almost to be double jointed. He had a habit of gesticulating with his hands that was reminiscent of oriental culture. 'Another class that draws a lot of patients is the music appreciation session. Each week, a few people bring in a tape of their favourite music. They get to play a track and then discuss why they like it, how it makes them feel.'

'Right, I think I've got a fair idea of the day programme, then,' Maud assured him, intent on reaching the open air.

'I'll just show you round some of the rooms then, shall I?' suggested Jeremy as he stood up, shaking down his trouser legs with a wiggle.

Maud followed him once more down the corridor. She noticed that some of the paintings hanging were very poorly executed. It seemed patronizing to show such weak efforts. Other patients had much ability in this field, however, and there were some painted fish on one wall made from clay. Overgrown with seaweed and colour, their vibrancy lent them a sense of movement.

Some of the rooms, mostly empty, that they passed had odd

names; Quiet Room, Community Room, Willow Kitchen, and so on. Jeremy pointed them out as they passed, omitting, Maud was relieved to see, the Ladies' Toilet.

As they neared the Quiet Room, Maud glanced in and saw a row of people seated, similar to the row that she had taken her place in when she arrived. They were obviously patients; one could tell from the way they sat, upright, shrouded in the smoke that billowed from several cigarettes, their fixed gazes always ahead. There was no communication, and not even, as the room suggested, any peace.

'As you can see, it's quite a small set up.'

'Very cosy,' Maud remarked, coming to a standstill by his side.

'I'd be pleased if you would come in, say tomorrow, to attend a few of the classes. Whichever ones you want, of course.'

Maud shook her head definitely. 'I really don't think I want to come here.' She didn't know quite how to express herself so as to indicate that she had thought the matter through. However, she was adamant.

'But what happens if you have a relapse?' Jeremy wanted to know. 'It would make you feel a lot less isolated if you had somewhere to come.'

She thought back to the rowed patients, a seam of men and women, staring ahead, fixed not even on the passing Jeremy and Maud. 'I'll be fine,' she told him, pushing back the cuticles of her left fingers with the other hand.

'Well, give me a ring tomorrow, to say yes or no either way,' was his response, unwilling to give up hope.

She didn't want to offend. 'I'll do that,' she answered, sounding slightly hopeful for his benefit. After all, she did want to get out of here. 'Thanks for showing me around, I appreciate it,' she concluded, smiling with relief that she was to be let loose. 'Not at all,' he added with a flourish of his hand, directing her to the open door, 'I hope to see you soon,' and then she was gone, as instantaneously as she had arrived, once more out of King George's and into the free air. She breathed in deeply, negotiating the petrol fumes of the traffic outside.

Eventually, however, Maud was persuaded to attend the community meetings at the day centre. It was of her own persuasion, commonly understood as curiosity, that she left the house at 8.15 each morning, allowing herself a full forty-five minutes for the journey.

Those first few mornings, her awareness of the surroundings along the route grew. A whole new understanding of the street life gradually developed, as previously when she had allowed herself an obsession with the Earl's Court roads.

Although there was nothing as outstanding as Hotel 167 on this route, a group of smaller symbols amassed in her mind and these served to protect her and give her superstitious guidance; the Michelin building, the man cleaning the pedestrian strip outside the McDonald's at the end of her road at the same time each morning, and the cake of the lady in a boulangerie window; these were her icons, though this time she kept them in perspective. Simply, she smiled when she met these things. In Israel, in Jerusalem, it had been the water hydrants that had trapped her attention. At every street corner and sometimes in between, these bright yellow double-headed monsters grew, similar to those of New York. It was more likely that this brand were in reality periscopes; periscopes used for underground surveillance. Thus it was that Maud developed an affinity with the vehicle of the same colour, parked in the grounds of King George's. It was a three-wheeler, used to tow a wooden cart, and for its nose there was a Perspex headlight, almost a medal. Its yellow was identical to that of the water hydrants, a pacifying colour despite the intensity.

After a cigarette in the dining room of the in-patient ward, Maud took a seat by the window in the community room. Some days a whole circle of members was formed, on other occasions there weren't the requisite three staff members to proceed with the meeting. Each day, a different patient assumed the task of chairperson and commenced with the identical formalities: 'Hello, and welcome to the community meeting. Could everyone please introduce themselves and say whether they are patients attending during the day, or in-patients.'

At this point Maud would feel her abdominals tighten, for the prospect of enforced speech always worried her. She would repeat her title inwardly as the mantra of names circled the room. And 'Maud Faulkes – out-patient,' she would finally blurt out, as unconcerned as possible.

'Are there any notices, or has anything happened since the last meeting that members should be made aware of?' was the next suggestion, frequently passed over.

The meeting was then 'opened for general discussion', and thence followed a silence of anything from a few seconds to ten minutes until someone found it in them to speak. Maud never said anything. She listened to others who talked of how they felt and questioned others on this same subject. Sometimes lewd jokes were made and laughed at, but even then the laughter was not natural. It was deep, forced, hysterical. Amanda, a slenderly stooping seventy-year-old, unaged because of her fine bone structure, might find it necessary to leave. When she did, she would politely inform the chairperson, haul herself up from her seat and urge her steps towards the door. The bang it made as she slammed caused the clock on the wall to shudder, and the remaining members to curl.

'Dr Fry wants to get inside my knickers,' Miriam stated that day, uncrossing her legs and reaching for her handbag at her feet. This she opened and pulled out a pre-wrapped packet of disposable handkerchiefs. She looked into one as she unfolded it, waiting for a response.

Dr Fry was Maud's GP and she remembered having seen two photographs of his young daughters on the wall of his surgery. It was at these photographs that she concentrated her gaze as he tapped her information into his word processor before issuing her with a repeat prescription.

'He's married, Miriam,' she told the woman, who was by now emptying and sorting the contents of her bag into her lap.

'Is he? Oh.' Her voice was completely passive, a heavy monotone laced with a nasal quality.

'Then it's adultery,' she resumed. Maud remained silent. Maud studied Martha's figure. She wore jeans and a sleeveless vest. Completely fleshless, nor did she shave underneath her arms, although her thin frame rendered this acceptable. For some reason skinniness and odourlessness seemed synonymous. She wondered how old Martha was. She looked like a teenager and seemed obsessed with the fact of having children. Although she had none of her own, she lived with her sister's and took responsibility for all the in-patients in the hospital, thereby bestowing great parental duties on herself. Whenever she became upset, her South London accent transformed to a soft Scottish lilt and it was ominous that she would then leave the room. Maud herself often felt the urge to leave. On this day there were few people present and she felt no inhibitions in doing so.

111

'I'm going out to have a cigarette,' she spoke to the chair-person as she stood up and made her way to the door. It was against regulations to smoke for the duration of the meeting and the hour was long and stressed.

'Maud, don't leave,' she was challenged with, but she did not stop in her tracks.

'I'll come back afterwards, then.' She reached for the handle.

'If you go out you're not allowed to come in again,' she was told.

Closing the door behind her, Maud was released from the pressures of the room, the pressure of not being able to leave and of having to calculate when to go against this rule. Outside there were several patients who also had left their meetings midway. One of them was Alexander, a man that she had first met when she was waiting for an out-patient's appointment with Dr Richards.

'Hi.' She walked towards him, offering a cigarette. He took one from the packet and she did the same. Producing some matches from his breast pocket, he lit one that was in fact two, held together by the brown tar that matches were dipped in. Maud inhaled from the light and sat down next to him. She had spoken to Alexander quite a lot since her attendance at the hospital. She liked the way that his black hair grew, forwards and slightly to one side.

'Coffee at ten,' she said, looking at his hairline. As he ran his hand absently over his hair, a sprinkling of white flecks flew from his scalp.

'You've got dandruff,' she noted.

He grinned. 'I know.'

One of the nurses, a Filipino lady dressed in a white lab coat, passed them by.

'Why aren't you two in your meetings?' she wanted to know.

'We're not allowed back in,' Alexander replied for the both of them. 'We came out for a cigarette and were told we had to stay out.'

'Well, you're both completely irresponsible, then,' she scolded shaking her head and walking past them into the office.

'Let's go into the garden.' Alexander got up and tilting his head sharply to the side made his way down the corridor, pushing through the swing door at the end.

The air was fresh, completely unlike the disinfected smell of the in-patients' ward where the community meetings were held. There, there was always a green-dressed cleaner, bending over the floor, with a mop and a stainless-steel bucket of detergent. The detergent was lemony but it made Maud feel nauseous. There was something overly sweet about it that grasped at your nostrils.

There were plenty of flowers in the gardens. Beautiful rose bushes that had opened up fully now. The best ones were pale pink with yellow edging round the petals and at the centre. 'Pick me a flower,' she asked and Alexander crossed over to the bush. He tore off a stalk and held it out to her. She took it, sniffing deeply at its heart, and then secured it in the buttonhole of her dress.

Maud's relationship with Alexander was unquestionable. She herself never thought about it and he was too ill for it really to have meant anything. Simply, they had on occasions enjoyed each other's company as did the whole of the community in the psychiatric unit. Only once, when they had decided to venture into a mental health group meeting, had this led her into trouble.

As, sitting, they formed part of the ubiquitous patients' circle, Maud had inadvertently, or at least without enough thought, slipped her hand underneath Alexander's belt, allowing it to rest on his stomach. He was slouched in his chair so that his trousers reached a much higher point of his body than when, standing, they dragged at his hips. Both of them had participated fully in the group and Maud had not been awaiting any trouble. At the end of the meeting, however, one of the male nurses asked to speak to her privately. With faint dread, she followed him to the office, watching his posture assume the importance of authority, his shoulders setting to military alignment. This was only successful from behind because facially he was adolescent with several permanent pimples and eyes set too close together. He held the door open for her and stood squarely towards her in the office. She saw how much taller than herself he was and hoped for leniency. His name was Floyd.

'I don't care what you and Alexander get up to in your spare time,' he began, his eyes focusing on hers minutely and with indecent suggestion.

'We don't get up to anything.' She spoke in sincere defence.

'Well, it's none of my business what you do when you're not in the hospital,' he affirmed, 'but I think it's wholly inappropriate,' here his voice shook and he showed demonstrative anger in his bodily expressions, 'for you to have your hand down Alexander's trousers during one of the meetings.' He continued to stare.

'I understand,' was Maud's answer, and indeed she accepted his comments, though what she did not understand was why he had not mentioned the discrepancy earlier, sorted it out efficiently at the point of time when it had occurred.

'I don't expect anything like this to ever happen again, in

my presence or otherwise. Not while you're in the boundaries of the hospital,' he stated firmly, and she could tell that he was displeased that she had not tried to usurp his authority. She knew that, for him, she had been far too ready to accept her misbehaviour.

That incident had taken place a week previously and although it had shaken her up for some hours following, it was now forgotten, though embedded in her mind.

The respect that Maud had for Alexander stemmed from his understanding of her mind phases, most importantly his acceptance of Hotel 167.

Early on in their friendship, she had let slip that a whole year of her life had been lived through such experiences. Without having to explain the term that she herself had created, Alexander had instinctively known what she meant. 'Mind phases, I have them too,' was all that he had remarked and although they must have been the only two in the hospital who outwardly shared this phenomenon, he had not seemed pleased or surprised at her revelation. Maud was delighted though; she felt at once twinned with this man who, having been in hospital for countless years, had the physiognomy of a child.

For once Maud had found someone to whom she could preach the beauty of mind phasing. A needless form of preaching, because of course it was not now her only way of life. In fact Alexander became convinced that she, being the younger by eight years, was merely reliving his past experiences. He suffered from schizophrenia and gradually pieced together the notion that Maud had been implanted post-conceptually with some of his DNA, so that in fact she was a clone of himself.

Although she liked the idea of being so much a part of

someone else and while she agreed that this was feasible, Maud
disbelieved a great deal of what she saw as Alexander's fancies.
This in fact distanced her from him and meant that their
relationship could be no more intimate than those she shared
with the other patients. It was the illness that separated them;
his illness, and she grew to loathe it. So much so that she put
it out of her mind. To some extent, he went with it.

Hotel 167 had, however, been released. It was no longer
the figment that festered in her mind. Because it had been
accepted without question by someone else, recognized as
something completely normal, it was allowed to grow. It was
not Maud who allowed it that capability, it was something that
had been externally granted, in the same way that once an
animal survives its first few months, it has a greater chance of
living. As well as the right to do so.

Deserving of its self-importance, it was still necessary for
Hotel 167 to prove itself to higher powers. It had to be admitted
that Alexander being insane, its position in life was not yet
wholly secure. Grumer signified authority to Maud. Not pure
authority, earned by morals, but the stamp of authority with
the power to testify.

It was he who should be used to seal the corporeality of
Maud's former and most important mind phase. And in doing
so, he would inadvertently forgo the security of his own pro-
fession. At least, in as much as psychiatry could be seen as
something secure whilst philosophies and religions wavered. As
of yet, Maud was unsure whether she would or would not
allow Grumer to earn her. It would all depend on himself and
how he proceeded with his diagnosis of her. She knew herself
well enough to verify the correctness of his interpretations, and
she would not play psychological games with him on that level.

It would all be dealt with fairly so that if he wasn't ruled by any unethical motivation, he would be allowed her acceptance of him.

Maud's plan to meet Grumer at Lou Pescadou was, as before, dictated by the time that she had spent with Yasmin and Alan. She had called him up the previous day to set a time for their meeting.

She wore the same outfit that she had worn on the original date, her black slacks and colourful silk Pucci shirt. The shirt was of pinks and mauves, lending itself well to her slightly cream complexion. Her hair was not loose, as usual, but tightly bound into a French braid.

She arrived at the favourite porthole building, to find Grumer seated at the table at the back of the restaurant. She had told him that if possible that was where she wanted to sit. Whoever was to arrive first should bag the table. At Lou Pescadou's, of course, there was no advance booking, but the first come first served policy was relied on. This meant that the restaurant was always thriving, as it was that particular night, a Thursday.

Grumer stood up as she came towards him and the waiter held her chair as she settled herself at the table. He handed them the menus, only to have them waved away by Maud.

'Two orders of oysters please, and a bottle of your excellent 1989 Pouilly Fumé. It's a great accompaniment to the seafood,' she added for the benefit of Grumer.

The waiter left their table with an inclination of his head and once more the two of them were alone.

'Why oysters?' Grumer demanded.

'Don't you know?' Maud teased. 'I do hope you like oysters.' She extricated the pressed linen napkin from her wine glass and slid it instinctively across her knees. 'Even if you don't, they are necessary for this stage of our meeting,' and she watched Grumer's eyes for recognition.

'Ah,' he observed, 'you came here with your two friends, your foster parents,' he added, taunting. 'That was the riddle?'

'Perhaps.'

The waiter returned with the bottle of wine, which he proceeded to uncork at the table, pouring first a small measure for Maud to taste. She lifted her hand and, understanding immediately, the waiter filled both of their glasses decently.

'Try the wine,' she offered and Grumer took a sip, wincing slightly with concentration.

'A good choice,' he approved, and Maud downed her first glass. They did not speak until, minutes later, the plates of food arrived, a dozen opened oyster shells, the greyish meat neat as a woman's labia.

'I know what you're thinking,' Maud confessed to him, watching as he eyed the food.

'And you are too,' he completed, with a wry laugh.

'Of course, what else are oysters for,' and after toying the toe bar with the prongs of her fork, she held the first shell to her lips, sucking. Swift as anything, the food shot down her throat, for she was not a slow gulper, as Grumer was. He took his time, first sucking the juices from the shell and then tipping his head right back so the oyster caught the back of his throat as it descended.

He licked the sauce from his lips. 'Luckily, oysters are my favourite,' he told her, picking up the second freed shell, 'especially when I'm not paying,' he grinned.

'Oh, but you are,' he was told, 'it's only fair that you should stand me a meal after what I'm about to reveal to you.' She hinted.

They were oblivious to the throngs at the other tables. They had been lucky in their choice, for it stood slightly apart from the rest of them.

'Well, begin then,' he demanded, agitation showing in his voice, his eating habits slowing, as he stifled a burp and brought the napkin to his lips. It had crumpled immediately in his great cumbersome hand, and he threw it down before bringing the wine glass to his lips once more.

'I've told you about Alan and Yasmin,' she began, watching as, interested, he nodded, coaxing her on.

'Well, we came to this restaurant, and, as today, we ordered oysters. Except we asked the waiter to bring us three orders on one large plate.'

Grumer raised his eyebrows, surprised at their combined ingenuity.

'What happened?' he asked.

'We went round anti-clockwise, first Yasmin, then me and then Alan. Yasmin prised the first one from its shell and then, as I held my head back, let it slide down my throat.' She demonstrated, relishing the peristaltic movement of her oesophagus, so close to an orgasm.

'Then it was Alan's turn, and I prepared two for him. You see, Yasmin and Alan always ate two because they never fed each other.'

Grumer looked at her, puzzled, and she elucidated.

'I would feed one of them twice, they would feed me once, then I'd feed the other twice and be fed once by that person. So in actual fact, we ate in twos and Yasmin and Alan never got to feed each other.

'If you'd seen them, you would have understood. They wanted each other so badly. When Alan turned away, he was actually unable to look at her, she slid across and tipped one down his pants. You should have seen his face.' At this point she laughed freely.

Grumer looked on, disconcerted by what she had told him. 'In the middle of the restaurant?'

'Come on, it was like tonight, absolutely packed, no one noticed what we were doing and to be honest I don't think that they would have cared one way or the other. Where's your sense of humour?' she joked, lifting one of her oysters to his lips. At first he drew back, but she persisted, and he didn't want the garlic and herb sauce all over his suit; it was easier for him to comply with her wishes. Tilting his head, he enjoyed the slippery sensation once again, half wishing that he had been part of their group before.

'Do you like Parma ham?' Maud asked suddenly, grinning at Grumer's embarrassment.

'Yes, and you?'

'I love it. Want to know why?'

Grumer nodded.

'I think out of all the foods that exist on this planet, it has to be the most sexual and sensual that there is.' She paused. 'Well, maybe oysters are more sensual. I'd say sexual, then. Hasn't it ever crossed your mind?'

Grumer shook his head. He was growing perturbed, the flush that had begun at the root of his beard was spreading more widely now, and the tips of his ears burned crimson. He didn't like the confined but public setting for their meeting. He wondered if the choice had been deliberate. An attempt at his discomfort. But then he let pass this idea. Hadn't Maud taken him there because that was where she had come with Alan and Yasmin? She was trying to recall the events for him as realistically as possible. Mind you, there were plenty of other restaurants and bars that they must have been to. 'To me Parma ham is just like a hymen,' Maud explained. 'Only when it's cut so fine so that it's transparent,' she added. 'And the smoky smell too, so powerful. What do you think?'

Grumer said nothing, then, 'I really hadn't thought of it in that way before, but I can see what you mean. I shall enjoy my Parma ham all the more in future for that exciting interpretation.'

Grumer breathed deeply. He was beginning to feel turned on; he must not let this child get to him in such a way. He was the one who was in control and they were both aware of that fact. Grumer. The psychiatrist. Someone who could understand and explain everything that Maud thought or said. Except that he couldn't, though in his mind he should have been able to. He sighed. 'Parma ham,' he said, aloud.

'Oh yes,' said Maud. 'Then Yasmin unbuttoned the fly of my trousers. These ones, you see they do up with a series of buttons,' and she indicated these to Grumer, who was in a state of shock.

'On the end of her fork, she had spiked an oyster. The prongs of the fork did not quite go through the meat,' she explained. 'She held the oyster to my clitoris, you have to try it, of course though you don't have a clitoris,' she joked. 'Does your wife like clitoral or penetrative stimulation?' she now asked, quite seriously.

'I don't know, I'm not sure,' Grumer stammered, trying to control himself. He was beginning to feel the sweat trickle down his back. Not only that, but he could feel the heat rising from beneath his collar.

'Well, that is something you should know. How long have you been married?'

'Fifteen years.'

Maud gave a low whistle. 'Fifteen years. And how often do you sleep together?'

'Whenever, I don't know, I've never counted.'

'I see,' she teased, 'you imply that if you wanted to, though, you could.'

'You were saying something,' he reminded her, trying to detract from the present line of questioning.

'Ah yes, she held the fork to my clitoris, two juicy bits of meat in contact with each other. Divine. Rolling the oyster gently over my clitoris – hey you did ask me if I masturbated when we first met,' she laughed, eyeing his discomfort. He made an effort to smile, though the corners of his mouth were dried with oyster juice. He rubbed the gummy stuff from the crannies. 'Anyway,' she continued, 'I came in the restaurant. It was the most perfect orgasm.' Reaching across, she felt for Grumer's fly, pronging an oyster with the fork in her other hand, 'Come on, give it a try, I'll be careful, you won't find yourself circumcised . . . or are you already?'

'That's my business.' Grumer was pleased that he had found something to hold on to, to prolong her interest in him. Perhaps later on she would try to find out. She seemed to have the traits of a nympho, should he tell her? Best not, if he did she might get offended, more likely she'd just laugh, but then make a point of fending him off if he made any advances. Just to prove her point. She was tough like that.

'I did the same thing to Yasmin, and Alan watched her come. We used a different oyster, you see she wanted to eat the one that gave me the orgasm. Said the sauce hadn't been salty enough.'

Grumer cringed within himself.

122

'Alan was looking really jealous there for a moment, so we let Yasmin give him one. It was the first time that they had touched each other properly for days, you know. That was part of our plan. And it wasn't at all easy for Alan at that point. I think women are much more likely to be silent when they come. I think that's what the turn on was for me and Yasmin. Knowing that if we didn't suppress ourselves, the whole restaurant would find out. Would we have been thrown out, I wonder? Maybe they would have made us do the dishes, as an excuse for us to go behind the scenes and do a round up of all the chefs and waiters.' Maud laughed. 'We shared Alan's oyster, now that one really was sauce ridden. Full of protein you know.' Her voice was not serious, its tone instructive.

'I'm sure,' Grumer supplied.

'Well, that's about it,' Maud finished, getting up to leave.

'Where are you going?' she was asked.

'I have to go now, but I'll give you a call later in the week.' Turning to leave, she caught the waiter's eye.

'The meal was lovely, thanks' – she handed him a five-pound note, enjoying the shine that this gesture lent his eyes – 'the gentleman is paying,' and then she was out of the building and into her precious fresh air.

Maud had never been able to understand the importance of freedom to her. Wherever she was, if it was indoors she felt trapped. She seemed to have a leaning towards exits, although she could never have lived in the country; she would have died of boredom. She needed the people of the large city, although she was at the same time wary even of her own family. She thought that perhaps that was what London did to people, made them hate and need at the same time. Just in the same ways as a baby can detest and want for its mother simultaneously.

It hated the mother because it was inherently aware of the desertion to be experienced, particularly if male. Surely male babies twigged at some point that it wasn't completely wholesome to suckle at their mother's breasts. At the same time, they craved the milk, were dependent on this parent to be supported and looked after, though they never knew when they were to be finally cast away, like a garment suddenly found to have been outgrown. It was a sad affair.

'At the cemetery was the next chapter,' began Maud, as she and Grumer were seated below one of the stone arches. 'On more than one occasion we spent the day in Brompton Cemetery, smoking marijuana,' she elucidated, watching as usual for Grumer's reaction.

He raised his eyebrows: 'I've warned you about marijuana before,' was his response, 'it's a more powerful drug than people believe. Its over use can induce schizophrenia.'

'I'm already taking tranquillizers for schizos,' Maud complained, looking at the several hairs that sprouted from the arch of his nose. When she looked closely, she could see the individual pores of his reddened skin, enlarged and angry. 'Of course they wouldn't admit to me that I was schizophrenic, but I know I've a split personality. Some days I just can't control myself.' A sudden downcast expression moved across her face, hardening the features.

'Maud, my dear, there is no possibility of your being schizophrenic.' He half smiled, half sighed. 'Psychotic, yes; schizophrenic, no.'

She grinned. 'Well, that certainly is a great reassurance,' she said, hopping down from the wooden bench on which she had been seated, cross-legged.

From the pocket of her jeans, she produced a small tin. Lifting the lid, inside was to be found a matchbox, a pack of king-size Rizlas and a few loose matches.

Grumer looked into the tin. 'Why don't you keep the

matches inside the box,' he asked, 'they'll get damp and then they won't strike. Besides, I thought you didn't smoke, filterless are the strongest that you can get.'

Maud laughed, pushing open the matchbox. Inside, on a bed of tobacco was what looked like half an Oxo cube. Striking a match and holding the resin in the warmth of its flame, Maud let it soften, before crumbling half of the substance into the tray of tobacco. Kneeling on the ground and using a rung of the bench as a table, this she sprinkled on to a cigarette paper, before moistening the gummed edge with the tip of her tongue. With a flash of her fingers she skinned up the joint, twisting the end of the paper and tearing it off between her teeth. *Pfff*, she spat the tip out and pushed the joint between her lips.

'Marijuana,' Grumer said.

Maud nodded as she lit the second match, holding the end of the joint in its flame as she inhaled and puffed out before taking a long deep drag. This she held in her lungs for about a count of ten, before the grey smoke curled from her lips and jettisoned downwards from her nostrils. Offering it to Grumer, he took it awkwardly. 'In the sixties we used to dose massively on marijuana,' he revealed.

'And did you become schizo?' she asked, eyebrows raised in question. Shaking his head, he drew from the cigarette, leaning back on the hard dark bench, letting his legs rest their length in front of him.

Maud was once again sitting next to him. She felt a queer sensation. It was as if, when she shut her eyes, she was moving backwards. She knew however that her body remained quite still.

'Tell me about the time you spent here with Yasmin and Alan,' was his request, and handing her the joint he waited as she sucked inwards, held for ten and repeated the process.

'I love the smell . . .' She paused, beginning, 'Yasmin had been to Russia the year before we met. While she was there, she happened on a large bush of weed. She couldn't believe her eyes at first, but then she decided she would take some and bring it into England on her return. She picked about fifty leaves, she took a cutting as well, but it died a few weeks after she planted it. Anyway, Yasmin pressed the weed between the pages of a book. One whole book filled with leaves. When she got back to England they had dried out and she had a fair supply. Enough to last her almost a year; she hardly smokes the stuff. Alan likes it, you see, and besides it was there for the taking, what else could she do. Ignore it?'

Grumer shook his head. 'All the same,' he said, 'it was a bloody stupid thing to do, especially in a country like Russia. If she had been caught . . .' He let out a low demonstrative whistle.

'Well, it's a good thing she wasn't. I made her promise never to do it again. Shame it's so hard to get your hands on weed in England. In America they actually have a shortage of resin.'

'One of the reasons you want to live there?' he asked facetiously.

Maud snorted. 'You just have no idea, do you?' She spoke in a garrulous tone, mocking, almost a sneer.

'Well, we decided all to meet up here one day. That was one day of many. Alan and Yasmin rolled up six or seven joints and we smoked them one after the other.' By this time the joint had burned down to her fingers. She threw it on to the ground, stamping at the red burn dot and scattering ash. 'Of course, I smoked one too many. With leaves, there's a gradual build up, and we didn't leave long enough between them for our bodies to assimilate the drug. I began to get the most frightful head rushes. So bad that I had to lie down on the grass.' She laughed at the memory, embarrassed slightly. Grumer said nothing, he listened intently.

Maud wondered whether he got turned on by details of her exploits. She glanced down at his crotch. Nothing.

'Yasmin and Alan began necking wildly while there was I, completely laid out. They began to worry about me, said that I had gone as white as a ghost. Even my lips were bloodless.' She sensed Grumer edging towards her and slid off the bench and on to the cool stone below.

'My parents' office is in Earl's Court and all I could think of as I looked up in their direction was that I wished they would come and collect me. Look after me until the head rushes passed. Every time I opened my eyes, the sky was swimming above me. It was a ludicrous thing to happen. I really should have known my own limits. You see I wasn't used to smoking as heavily as the other two.'

Grumer joined her, dusting the ground with a large linen handkerchief before entrusting the seat of his suit pants to it. Maud noticed and had to restrain a sneer of repulsion at his behaviour.

'Maybe they had sex there and then, I couldn't know. I was felling too ill. They made me feel guilty about it afterwards. Said that I was the one who was to keep my wits about me. As mediator, my duty was to separate them, the veritable gooseberry. I was to ensure the platonic side of their relationship, not to let them become physically overwhelmed by each other. I failed.'

'Did it matter so deeply?' Grumer asked. Another of his failings; he just didn't have the subtlety to imagine what there was between those three. Obviously he had never had such a delicate relationship in his life. Maud edged away and began picking at the green mossy growth of one of the tombstones in front of her.

'They teased me,' she continued, 'they ate Turkish Delight together. "Give some to Maud," I heard Yasmin say, and when I opened my eyes Alan was leaning over me. Instinctively I took the blossoms that he held in one hand, although in the other was my intended sweetmeat. It became a long-standing joke . . . The flower having been for Yasmin,' she added.

'Then something terrible happened, something that began our downfall. The others were superstitious. They had had our charts drawn up and were always mapping the ongoing cycles. Yasmin used to do our combined Tarot cards.'

'And?' Grumer hurried her on, impatient as ever.

'Alan stood up, he jumped down from where we're sitting now, supporting himself on one of those tombstones.' Now she pointed to a white cross that appeared to be made of chalk. Maud read his thoughts. 'Yes, it looks like chalk, doesn't it,' she said, 'and it is. Or something similar. The whole thing crumbled into nothing.' She shivered as she spoke. 'It put the dampers on the day, and when we were about to leave, I climbed over a grave, and slipped and fell, crash, right on to it.' There was something detectably strange in Maud's voice as she spoke. 'Nothing was the same afterwards. We felt that there was an evil, an omnipresence. We just couldn't continue in the same carefree way.'

Maud curled her bottom lip under her top front teeth. She moistened them and leant over to Grumer, kissing him on the cheek. Impulsively, he put his hand out to her breast, his breath quickening heavily, until he had forced himself down the front of her boat-necked top. She shuddered and drew away quickly, lightening the situation by throwing him a scattering of green quartz-like stones from one of the graves.

'Don't do that!' His voice came sharply now, for he had respect for the dead. 'Something will happen if you behave badly in a cemetery,' and he began to collect the small green stones, returning them to their verdigris bed.

'Return to the cemetery,' mouthed Maud as she met Dr Grumer outside Earl's Court station.

He smiled at her, slightly bemused, and nodded enquiringly at the wicker basket that she held in her left hand. Ignoring this, 'I couldn't make the same mistake that I made with Yasmin and Alan,' she explained, taking him by the suited arm and leading him down Earl's Court Road. 'We never returned to the cemetery after the frightening incident with the tombstones.' Turning to him, she grinned, 'I feel this need to exorcize myself there now; you're a shrink, you understand these things.'

'But am I becoming closer to understanding you?' was his reaction, and she cringed inwardly at the fondness that she detected in his eyes. It was an expression that she occasionally recognized in Alexander's features, but her response to him was always one of gratification.

'You will after today,' she replied, 'or perhaps you won't. It's as if we're at the fulcrum now. We might tip either way; exciting, isn't it?' And she looked down at the basket, rearranging the checked linen cloth that covered its contents. 'You know, when I was preparing our picnic,' she emphasized these words in revelation, 'I mind phased myself into "Boule de suif". I wanted everything to be exact. Just as Maupassant would have wanted. Only we'll both eat. Kind of.' Laughing, 'Maybe it's closer to "Boule de suif" than I had thought of,' she added and they stepped up their pace. Now they were at the junction

131

where Earl's Court Road meets Old Brompton Road and it was here that they crossed.

'You didn't pass Hotel 167 on your way?' Maud asked.

Grumer shook his head. 'I'm saving myself for you to make the introduction. Something I'm very much looking forward to.' Again the glint in his eye.

'What do you mean?' she asked with the indignant innocence that she felt. The time was crucial and she feared that the balance might tip for the worse. But Grumer said nothing, looked straight ahead, though there was a perceptible smirk at the edges of his lips, almost disguised by the wiriness of his beard.

It was not long before they arrived at the cemetery gates. As usual, the main entrance was locked, so they made their way through the smaller wrought-iron one at the side. Ahead of them, the long stretch that led to the arches, edged with the tips of the tombstone fields.

'So, we're having a picnic,' Grumer remarked searchingly; 'it's lucky I haven't eaten.'

'I'm sure you would have found room.' Now Maud linked her arm with his. 'Besides, it's only half twelve.'

'You plan everything in advance, don't you?' His look, she was pleased to see, was now one of benevolence; the father proud of his child's peculiarities.

'I'm kind of manipulative, I guess. At least that's what my parents used to tell me.'

'But weren't they, as well?' was Grumer's response.

'All parents are, I think. They have to be, especially if they don't want to punish their children physically.'

At the centre of the cemetery there were arches on either side. Maud guided the psychiatrist to the row on the left-hand side and they weaved through the tombstones to be near it.

Once seated by some steps that looked over the back of the cemetery, Maud pulled the basket towards her. 'Food,' she said as she lifted off the red and white cloth. 'Simple fare,' she elaborated, pulling out the white rolls and wrapped cheeses. 'A ploughman's lunch.' Grumer helped himself to the bread and made his choice from the assortment of cheeses; Brie, Cheddar, Edam, Roquefort.

Maud hooked her legs in the nook behind the pillar nearest to her and tore open one of the rolls. It was sprinkled with poppy seeds and she filled it with a chunk of Brie, seared from the wedged triangle.

'What now?' Grumer asked, looking across at the variety of tombstones. He was attracted by a family tomb, crowned with four angels, most of which had lost their limbs through time. 'Time will tell,' Maud bit into her sandwich. 'Do you like Maupassant?' she asked.

'And were your parents manipulative?' came the retort.

Laughing, and then shrugging, she concentrated on the creamy taste of the Brie and the nuttiness of the seeds. 'Chewing's hard work,' putting the last of the bread into her mouth, she dusted her hands together and threw the crumbs from the skirt of the dress that she wore.

'You didn't say anything about my dress.'

Grumer looked her up and down. 'That's because you expected my reaction,' he revealed.

'And you know me so well,' she finished.

'I think so.' He sounded a little unsure and busied himself with the contents of the basket, breaking off a chunk of Cheddar cheese which he ate on its own, like a mouse.

'Well, can we have no more questions then?' she asked of him. 'It's make or break time. We've either made it or we haven't.'

Grumer didn't look up, merely continued to chew. 'No more questions about parents or lovers, then,' he replied. 'Or sex, or self, just no more questions.'

Maud sighed, 'I'm spent,' and she dug deep into the basket, extracting a couple of cans of beer. Handing one to Grumer, she pulled at the ring of her own, enjoying the fast release of the gases inside. Drinking thirstily, she emptied half the can in one go, wiping her mouth with the back of her hand before burping deeply from the pit of her stomach.

'At least you're dressed like a lady,' Grumer joked and she smiled silently.

She lay down and the two of them were silent for several minutes. Then as quickly, she rose to a sitting position and reached into the side pocket of her dress.

'Now it's time for the interval,' she said, producing from the pocket a waxy wrapper. Grumer glanced at her hand from which she withdrew a fresh Wilkinson razor blade. He did not speak. Silently he watched as Maud lifted her right arm, the one already covered in a multitude of scars.

Taking the blade between finger and thumb of her left hand, she concentrated as she drew the blade deeply across the unveined side of her arm. First, simply a score; and then the score filled; it was as if the white line was crying, crying blood, first in little tears and then filling to a tiny trench that bled loosely.

Still Grumer remained silent and Maud continued. Line after line. Rescoring those scars as if guided by a transfer. There was no expression on her face as she proceeded with her work.

Inside she felt no emotion. The expurgation that was there was simply a factual one.

The blood ran beautifully down Maud's arm, rendering sleek her hairs. Looking at the small scene that she had created she was satisfied to see on herself, a human, the colours of an animal. Why were we so dully cast, none of the dusting of birds or the prints of cats, no fur nor even a tail?

She wiped the wet blade between her fingers, drawing on to them the excess blood, then let it drop to the ground. It made a tinny clatter.

'And for the finale?' Grumer appealed to her in wonder, amazed that she would carry on in front of him, too amazed to have stopped her, not knowing through years of experience when or when not to show reaction.

Pulling herself to her feet, Maud bent forwards slightly and lifted her bloodied arm to her mouth. Three times she forced her first two fingers down the back of her throat, gagging and feeling the rise in her stomach. Then with release, the food that she had eaten, frothed with the beer she had drunk, was expelled on to the grass below the ledge on which she stood. Wiping her mouth with her hand, she looked at Grumer. 'No more,' were her words. 'That's it,' and she left him at the cemetery to walk back alone. Speechless until their next meeting.

The message on Grumer's answerphone was to meet Maud at Hotel 167, in the room that she had taken.

When he arrived at the hotel, he announced himself at the registration desk and was given the spare key as requested by Miss Faulkes.

Making his way up the stairs, he knocked on the door to make his presence known to her, before inserting the key and letting himself in. At first, the room seemed empty save for a few belongings that Maud had brought with her; these were a small stack of books, primarily Anaïs Nin and Scott Fitzgerald, as well as a tall pottery vase painted in mottled shades of blue.

He had been in the room a few minutes before he heard the faint sounds from the bathroom.

The door was open and appeared at first to be empty. He soon realized the presence of Maud, slouched behind the door. Maud held an electric toothbrush to the pale mound of hair that was the surround of her vagina. Protruding from the reddened labia was a slim anti-perspirant aerosol which she handled rhythmically, moving it gently inside her.

'Come in,' she called to Grumer, undeterred by his presence, and he obeyed, taking his seat on the lavatory top.

'Maud,' he spoke her name reproachfully, causing her to giggle.

'Come on, Grumer, you asked me all that time ago if I masturbated. You were the first shrink to ask me that question. At the time I actually felt that you were doing it to test my reaction, to see me blush. What do you think?'

He smoothed his beard with the tips of his fingers, extricating a thin yellow filament of dried egg from one of the whiskers.

'Actually, I was trying to gauge your feelings with regard to sexuality,' he revealed, studying the drugged expression that her features bore. 'I suppose this episode is of relevance to your relationship with Yasmin and Alan?'

'Yes. The culmination,' she replied. 'I never saw them again following the long days that we spent together in this hotel.' Her expression was now clouded by these words.

'Alan would crouch behind me, supporting my arms in his hands, while Yasmin made me come, again and again. The toothbrush is wonderful, you should try it. Sometimes she used her tongue. I always feel insecure about oral sex. It's to do with the pubic hair;' Grumer grimaced and she went on: 'They both wanted so badly to please me, just like parents . . .'

'That was the riddle, wasn't it?' Grumer's voice was softened.

'What was?' she asked warily.

'Your parents. The key to your problems. Did they abuse you, is that it? Abuse you and then dump you, like Yasmin and Alan?' His voice grew gradually until it boomed loud. 'They did, admit it, won't you?'

'Nothing of the sort,' was the curt reply. 'Well, at least not physically. My, my,' she pondered, 'you psychiatrists have no charm, no delicacy of mind and no subtlety. Everything with you is ruled by sex, ruled by the lack of it. Absolutely no charm.' She was grown angry now, though only sarcasm was detectable in her voice.

'Maud,' he came closer, was kneeling next to her now, his mouth pressed to the cartilage edging of her ear, 'let me make love to you, you don't have to be alone.'

She switched off the toothbrush and set it down. Then she retrieved the can from within herself. It made a little suction noise as she brought it back to the open.

'Smell,' she offered and Grumer obeyed. He moved closer to her now so that she could feel his erect penis.

'It smells of golden syrup, doesn't it?' she said and he nodded. 'A faint frosting of golden syrup, slightly hairy,' she elaborated. 'But guess what!' and she passed her tongue over the thin layer of mucus, 'it's as salty as caviare,' and she held it to his tongue watching as eyes closed, he moved his lips round the aerosol as if round his own sex.

'Let me fuck you,' he repeated, moving on top of her, his hand at her breast, now at his zipper, now at her cunt.

'Get off,' she ordered, her voice the Germanic tone of a Führer, 'off, I said,' as if he were a dog round a bitch on heat, and she threw him off her as easily as if he were a sack of potatoes. He struggled up.

'Come on, you want it,' he pleaded, his eyes beseeching, taking her in fully.

'You fucker, you bastard,' she shouted, 'indelicate monster. Is that all you can think? Do you really believe that I would ever go with you!'

'Why did you ask me here, then?' he asked.

'Oh, to show you. But I've had enough now, so you can leave,' and picking up the blue vase she hurled it at him as he made for the doorway. 'You psychiatrist,' she muttered as she watched him go, as she ran to the window to see him leave the building. As she returned to her physical self-loving.